Fans are saying:

"We are impressed with the rawness of the author's voice. Her ability to weave her personal experience into her writing is unique. The book reaches all readers on different levels."

Booze & Books Club

"Wow, just wow! I felt like I climbed in the book and was enjoying the brunch, as well as joining the conversation with the characters.

LaTina M

"This is something that people can relate to, the hard parts of life that make you want to quit yet life goes on; I'm glad you told us how old jMarie is so women reading it will know that no matter how old you are, you can start living for YOU!

Stephanie

"Fantastic and funny - Incredible - Realistically Relatable - Strong- Tragically Triumphant

Lizetta Eve

"Really didn't want to read about "how" to make the sweet potato pie, but I did and my mouth is watering. Please just "send" me the pie. LOL"

I. M. Brown

I Need To See You Say

Anita Smith

Published by Anita Smith

ISBN 978-0-615-52716-1

In Loving Memory

My mother, Elizabeth "Bessie" Smith (8-9-1999)

My son, Jonathan "Jj" Arnold Brown, II (6-23-2000)

My sister, Lisa Beth "Pancakes" Smith (8-9-2008)

~~~~

Dedication

Carl Lancaster Smith, Sr. & (Elizabeth Smith- 1936-1999)
My 7 Sisters and 4 Brothers
My children, Jonathan (1975-2000) and Tinika
My grandchildren,
Breanna, Imani, Jonathan & Rae
and '4847' to ykw

~~~~

Acknowledgments:

I want to thank my heavenly father who gave me the working brain, knowledge and fingers to write/type this work of fiction after bringing me through some happy and some challenging life experiences and choices. Hallelujah! goes right there!

To my editors: Jazmyn's momma, Booze N Books book club, Barbara Lewis and my granddaughter Imani. If I used every page of the book my true appreciation still would not be evident of how grateful I am to each of you. With much appreciation, I say THANK YOU from the bottom of my heart.

Introduction

~~~~

This novel is about a mother (*jMarie*) who learns how to cope after doctors tell her that her twenty-five year old quadriplegic son (Jarvis) has about eighty days to live. It's about wondering where God was and if her faith or sometimes lack of faith, will really get her through the challenging times she would face.

With the help of her sister and friends she throws herself back into her invention world; which helps her get her life back on track. She then learns to take responsibility for her life and she pushes forward and moves on. Reversing the old saying "We live and we learn" *jMarie's* new motto is "Learning *then* living" because *you* still have life!

After re-emerging into her life and putting her School of Common Sense (SCS) degree back into action *jMarie* made about a half dozen New Year's resolutions, with the following four carried over from last year: 1) Stop giving advice to adults unless they are in an emergency situation and she is there to witness it. 2) Join Aliza's church (again). 3) Finalize the license for her invention and 4) Get a commitment from Vince or else.

Yes, *jMarie* is convinced this is going to be, not just a good year, but her year.

Contents

~~~~

The Call

... today is not the day you're expecting it.

The clock on the wall flips to 7:23, reminding me I've been here almost 12 hours. It is time to get the hell out of here and head to the airport. The Senator's flight arrives late tonight so I figure I may as well finish up the last of these travel orders.

Looking at the stack of completed travel orders I am beginning to wonder if there may be some truth to the complaints Senator Jane's constituents have been making lately. They say if she traveled less she may be able to accomplish more. But then again, what do I know, besides how to make arrangements and keep everything organized and on schedule? I must admit I can do a mean power point presentation.

Don't get me wrong, I'm not complaining, cause it pays to be a graduate of *School of Common Sense (SCS)* I don't know how many times I thought about just going ahead and getting a college degree, but my ass is too busy giving answers, advice and solutions to all the quote "college degree" folks that work with me.

I swear I am always repeating the same advice to everyone. I ask myself what's wrong with this picture. *One of these days, I'll wake up and make folks start thinking on their own two feet. I will stop giving them advice unless they are in an emergency situation and my ass is right there to witness it.*

Each day I understand more and more what my mother meant

when she said "If they don't have common sense, they don't have any sense." Boy is she right. I have to design that T-shirt "I wish *you* were a graduate of S.C.S."

Picking up the small mirror on my desk, I notice my makeup has left only traces of color on my face. With my two middle fingers and thumb, I begin fluffing my bangs…as if they were my own. Thank goodness tomorrow is payday, cause I sure need a new wig.

I saw Patti LaBelle looking good on TV the other night wearing a reddish blonde wig. Hmmm…note to self, *call 'It's 4Un4Me', and check on colors of "Patti LaBelle" wig collection.*

Damn my neck is killing me. Startled by the phone ringing, I jumped, my hand froze, and my fingernails dug deeply into my neck. Something inside of me was twisting and rumbling and in my gut I knew why. It was the call… the one you always feared you might someday get, yet today just is not the day you're expecting it. I pick up the phone and in the background I could hear the sounds of doctors being paged and patient's names being called. I could even hear the sound of an ambulance siren coming to a shirking halt.

"Hello"

"Ah, yes –um *jMarie*"

"Yes, it's me, is this you Aliza?"

"Um, yes it's, it's me.

Even though I could hear the police radios and a whole lot of other chatter, I did not think I heard my sister Aliza correctly, when she said,

"Jarvis been shot!"

"What did you say?"Then my sister repeated it.

"Jarvis been shot! He's in ICU. You have to get here."

There is a dead silence and I don't think I'm breathing, No,
I am almost sure I'm not breathing. Right in the middle of
all the background noise I heard when I picked up the phone. I
could see Jarvis there, lying on a stretcher, with a blood covered sheet
and doctors pushing that long metal pole with something dripping
through a cloudy yellow bag. I can see the nurses whispering "Hold
on—hold on" and of course I picture a cop trying to get all the info
he can, ignoring the fact that Jarvis may not make it. The whole TV
emergency room scene is rapidly flashing in front of me. My eyes are
stinging with sweat and tears. I feel numb, yet I can feel my entire
body shaking. I am not breathing.

Aliza must have thought I wasn't breathing either because I
could hear her yelling.

"Hello, Hello, Hel-lo, are you there?!"

"¡Marie, it's Aliza, answer me, are you okay? Say something."

Then she repeated it "Did you hear me? I said Jarvis been shot.
You need to get here"

My ears heard her; however, my mind was not registering three
of the words Aliza just said. Again my mind was blocked with the
TV scene of everyone running along side the stretcher, Jarvis not
saying a word. It was as if I was right there at the hospital, but I felt
helpless. I could not get near the stretcher because of all the doctors
and nurses. I couldn't touch him. I couldn't hug him I couldn't even
say, "Everything's gonna be alright."

Then I realized I could not do any of that because I wasn't there.
I wanted to run out of my office and head straight to the hospital,

forgetting I was over nine hundred miles away.

"*¡Marie*, you there?"

"Um, yeah I'm here," I scratch my head and scare the shit out of myself when my wig falls on my desk.

"Um, how? When? Ah where did this happen?"

"I don't have all the details. Dad just told me to call you and have you get here."

"Dad, he's there?"

"Yes, Nikita, Lydia, Dad and Vince are here. Someone will pick you up at the airport. Can you make your reservations, or do you want us to do it for you?"

"Wait, wait. How is he?"

Hoping the answer will be, he is fine, he will be okay, or he will make it. I wanted my sister's answer to be anything but "We don't know." My knees start shaking uncontrollably, like the nervous twitch I would get over forty years ago when I was in elementary school and I had a bad report card. It was that same exact nervous twitch that was always followed with that queasy stomach feeling and the words of "Wait till your father gets home"

It was that damn twitch that lets you know the worst is yet to come, and you cannot embrace or prepare yourself for it.

There is another question I want to ask. I'm scared to death to ask, it just will not come off my lips.

With each heartbeat, the fear grows of not knowing the answer to the unasked question, Instead of asking, I ramble on and on repeating all the other questions again.

"Where, When, How? Is his sister with him?"

"Yeah, Nikita is with him, I'll get her; she's in the ICU waiting room now. They are trying to calm her down because she has been yelling and screaming at the doctors, nurses, police, other patients, anyone in her path, not giving her the answers she wants. If she does not calm down, I'm afraid they are going to put her out, or all of us, as far as that goes, and then you know, there's no telling what she'll do.

Matter of fact, your friend, um, gosh what's her? The nurse"

"Lydia"

"Yes, Lydia"

"I saw I had several messages earlier today from Lydia, I was so busy, I just didn't pick up the phone.

Yesterday morning she left me a message something or other about she hit her elbow and it swelled up so bad she went to the ER. But later that night she left a message about knee surgery."

"That's Lydia, you know your friend."

"I swear she may be a nurse, but she has mixed up all those other degrees only to end up with an AHC."

"A-H-C? I thought Lydia was an RN."

"She is and she's a- hypo-chondriac. But enough of Lydia and damn her, I always threaten her that she's going to need me to pick up the phone and I won't someday.

"Well you know how Lydia is."

"Yea, but I didn't think the time I didn't take her call would be the time I was the one who actually needed it." she's always leaving so many silly messages. Today when I needed to...

"Sis, stop it.. You had no idea why Lydia was calling today?"

"I know sis, but."

"Lydia suggested we take Nikita to ER so they can give her something to calm her down. One minute Nikita is in complete control, next minute she's out of control. Daddy said she's little *jMarie*, acting just like you, and before you know it she'll flip the script, lose her professionalism, and then starts going off on everyone."

"Flipping the script and acting unprofessional is not me!"

"No, I didn't mean that part. We all know that's her dad in her."

"Really, you got that shit right, him or his evil ass mama"

"Speaking of her dad, did anyone call him?"

"No, do you want us to?"

"I'll decide that when I get to Tucson." Hell, don't anybody know how to get in touch with the sperm donor. He's the least of my worries right now.

"Hold on sis, Nikita is coming now. Nikita, your mom's on the phone."

"Wait sis, she stopping to talk to the nurse. Forget it, she's got one hand on her hip and she's waving the other all in the nurse's face, now she done snatched something off the counter, and knocked the plant off the nurses' station. Nikita, your mom is, "Hey sis, let me go see what the problem is, and I'll call you back."

Running down the hall, Nikita turns and yells back to Aliza.

"Aunt Aliza tell mom I love her and I'll call her as soon as I can, they need me back in ICU"

"Well sis, no need to call you back, 'because I can't go to ICU anyhow, Nikita told them that she is his sister and since she's mad at us right now. She said we are not allowed back; she won't even let dad back there.

"What do you mean she won't let anyone back there?"

"She's pissed off at us; she said no one called her"

"We explained to her that we did try to reach her, and then we called you. Everything was happening so fast, and we all got caught up in focusing on Jarvis."

"Of course, she wasn't trying to hear it; she made up her mind we didn't try hard enough to reach her."

"Enough of her; it ain't about her right now either. My head is splitting in two. Actually, it feels as if it's crumbling into pieces."

"Well, um…so where's dad? Let me talk to him"

"I'll go get him; I think he went outside"

"Outside?"

"Yes, he probably just wanted to get some air."

"It's strange, the police, doctors, nurses, even the rent-a-cop; everyone around us in authority, or who thinks they're in authority, are acting like they don't know anything. Yet they are all whispering and keeping their backs towards us as if they have some news they aren't sharing and we shouldn't know."

Tapping my fingers on my forehead, as if it will help me think, suddenly I slam the phone onto the receiver. My head feels as if it weighs a ton. I rest it between my hands. With my thumbs on my temples, I slowly massage my forehead with my other fingers. I close my eyes and try with all my might to squeeze out the last nine minutes of conversation I just had with my sister.

I picked up the photo on my desk of Jarvis and his sister. Until now, I had almost forgotten about the big, glassy teardrop about to slowly spill from his right eye. My mind drifts back to the day we had the picture taken, I clearly remember Jarvis was about to cry when the photographer asked me to step back and let him take a photo of just the two children. Jarvis, kept saying, "No, my mom has to be in the picture too." He kept saying "Huh mom, don't you have to get your picture taken with us, huh, don't you ma?"

The thought is making me smile through the pain right now.

I swear, when I blinked, his tear actually dropped in this picture along with my flood of tears I could no longer hold back.

With the palms of my hands I begin wiping my tears. I look down on my desk and the invoice I'm working on is soaking wet with tears. I pick it up by the only dry spot and get up to try to revive it so I can read it. It was so wet it ripped in half. I throw it on the desk.

"Damn it!. I have to get to my son. I have to get out of here.

I pick up the picture of Jarvis and Nikita again. I kiss the picture and place it face down on my desk because looking at it is making my heart stop.

My mind wanders back to the emergency room and I can just picture those folks, treating everyone like crap, And they think, Nikita is out of control. On second thought, I might be like Nikita and have to flip the script on them. They're damn lucky I'm not there at this moment. One thing I know for sure is I would have me some damn answers. Oh yea, somebody definitely would be sitting with me and my family giving us all the feedback as they received it. You can bet your bottom dollar on that shit!

"*jMarie, -- jMarie, jMarie,* pick up the phone"

"Hello? hello?"

I look over and suddenly realize the phone is off the hook, I pick it up.

"Hello"

"Damn, I thought I, I thought I hung up, Aliza I'm sorry I can't think, I'll need to call you back, please, just give me a minute."

"Okay"

"What's the number there?"

"Um, its area code 81 – oh wait, this pay phone does not receive calls, and it's been blocked from receiving calls. Probably too many dope dealers trying to return calls on it. Hold, on you'll have to call the hospital directly."

"Oh, wait, here comes your friend Lydia; let me get a number from her."

I sit back down and my leg begins shaking like crazy. Tapping my fingernails nervously on the desk, I spot my split nail and realize that's how my wig must have got caught. Mindlessly I pick up my wig and put it back on.

"*jMarie*, you there"

"Yeah,"

"The number is 816-424-1975; Lydia said she'll call you as soon as she has solid information for you.

"Oh, okay, thanks, tell Lydia I said to please take care of my son."

"Bye"

"Bye"

"Oh wait"

"Yeah"

"What hospital is he in?"

"Grant Road Medical "

"Oh, okay, bye."

"Love ya"

"Love you too"

The lump in my throat is so big I can't swallow. It feels as if someone has stuffed something in my throat to keep me from breathing. I feel a knife zigzagging through my heart. I'm trying to think, but I can't. I make a dash for the rest room.

Lucky for me it's at the end of this office. With my right hand pressing on my stomach in hopes to keeping me from throwing up. I open the door and can't even make it to the toilet; I begin throwing up in the sink. I can't stop the flow of tears and my stomach is twisting and turning so fast it's making my head, no my entire body spin. Suddenly I'm having déjà vu.

I'm telling myself, no not this feeling. . . God no, please, not again. But oh yes it is. It's the same exact feeling I had when the doctor told me my daughter, Nikita, who had just turned twelve, was pregnant. I had gotten so sick to my stomach, I thought my insides were going to come up to my throat and gag me to death.

I can see the doctor and the nurse who were both busy trying to hold Nikita down because she was kicking, and screaming at the top of her lungs, 'No! No! It's not true! It's not true mom! It can't be true!' I was thinking the same thing - -It can't be true. She was screaming and kicking so violently I thought she had gone insane. I remember it like it was yesterday. That moment made a firm believer in me that stress definitely brings on illnesses. Less than a month after that news, I was lying in the hospital recovering from ovarian cancer, which had been laying dormant for years; and no! Damn-it! No! It can't be true is haunting me again, ten years later. Only this time, the words were actually coming from my mouth. With my head still bent over the tiny restroom sink, I suddenly remember thinking how I was so against having them put this restroom right in my office. At this moment, I am ever so grateful for the facility.

I want someone to hold me, and hug me, but at the same time I'm kinda glad no one is in my office right now. Breathing hard, and at the same time trying to catch both my breath and my thoughts, I tell myself, "Relax, think of the water, blue skies, blue oceans," you know all that shit that a stress release class teaches you. Well, it ain't freaking working. There is no way I can concentrate on blue skies and oceans when my child needs me right now. But I do know what my ass needs to do is calm the hell down, get me some composure, and try as best I can to think straight; or at the very least *think*.

I want to stop throwing up, but I can't. As a matter-of-fact, I don't even remember eating enough food today to be getting this damn sick.

I never even heard the office door open, which explains why I almost jumped out of my skin when I heard "What are you still?"

My mind went completely blank and I couldn't even remember the name of Senator Jane's new intern as he stepped inside the door. "Damn, you look like you saw a ghost" he said. Spotting the sink, which just gave him more information than he bargained for, and one uncomfortable quick glance at my wig half off, he asked, "Did you… did you eat something that didn't agree with you?" can I get you some water?"

I could tell he was nervous by my appearance. With my hands, I tried to quickly fix my wig before bringing my head up from the sink. I fumbled for the box of tissues on the sink to wipe my mouth. I knock the box of tissues in the sink, "Damn-it" I reach up, pull a paper towel from the holder, and wiped my mouth. Holding my other hand up, I ask.

"Give me a minute please", I said it as if a minute was going to make everything all-right.

Like it was gonna make me think clearer.

Ump…to be honest, in that split second, it actually did just that, it made me think clear long enough to realize that I needed to get myself together. My son was definitely going to need his mom in her right frame of mind.

I was trying to hold back my tears, and look strong, I took a deep breath. I tried to swallow, but the fear that was caught in my throat was weighing down my chest as well.

"I just received a call that my son" . . . I swallow hard again and took another deep breath,

"My son"

"What- what about your son"

"He has been", I try to swallow, but it's caught in my throat.

"He has been shot."

"Shot?!"

"What? How is he?"

"I – I don't know? I have to call my sister back."

He came over, gave me a hug and said, "Go ahead call her, I'll be back in a few minutes."

He left me alone and I wanted to beg him to stay, but I couldn't. I just couldn't speak or think anymore, so I just cried hoping I could get all the tears out before he returned, before the intern could see me like this again.

~~~~

Calling on the Lord

*...it dawns on me that what I need to be stretching is my
faith, not this damn rubber band.*

Calling on the Lord is what I need to do. But something inside
me will not let me go into prayer at this moment.

I picked up the phone, and then I hung it up.

I picked it up again, and then hung it up again. My eyes
wandering over my desk looking for the hospital number my sister
had just given me.

I stared at the phone hoping it would ring. This time I wanted
my sister to say, "They made a mistake. They were wrong; it wasn't
Jarvis." I want her to say that it was someone else. I could deal with
feeling sorry for someone else's mother, someone else's child, a lot
easier than I could deal with this tragedy being my own. Lord knows,
if there's one thing I'm good at, it's being supportive to others. I start
to interlock the paperclips on my desk. Then I start lining up the
pens. Now placing everything in a straight row. Mindlessly, I am
lining my thoughts up. I pick up a stack of invoices, remove the
rubber band, and begin to stretch and re-stretch it. It dawns on me
that what I need to be stretching is my faith, not this damn rubber
band. I turned the photo of Jarvis and Nikita over, then put it back
down, then picked it up again, and began kissing it. I close my eyes
and I want to pray, but I do not know where to start.

Glad the intern has not come back, I started talking out loud to God, "Lord, I've sent up many prayers hoping this would never happen, tell me, why did I send you so many prayers if this is still the result, tell me Lord, tell me 'cause I'm sure as hell confused right now! Lord I beg you please do me a favor and keep my son alive please let me see him again."

Feeling guilty that my faith is weak at this time, I suddenly see my mother's handwriting at the bottom of every card she would give me and Aliza since we were little. She always wrote, "Remember now thy creator, in the days of thy youth." I find my thoughts hoping that I have given Jarvis enough faith and training in the days of his youth, hoping I've given him enough to know that the Lord can bring him through. I begin thinking about the days of Jarvis and his sisters youth. My mind takes me back to when I was raising them in a small town in Pennsylvania. Jarvis and his sister were singing in the Little Cherubs choir in which my no-singing-no-tune-no-rhythm self was the youth choir director. I couldn't sing, but those kids sure could. They were so good that me and my no rhythm, off beat tune never even fazed them. It was Easter Sunday, and Jarvis and Nikita were dressed up in their matching gray and white outfits. The Cherubs were singing (what is now Jarvis's favorite song) "We've Come This Far by Faith". When it was time for his sister to take the microphone and sing her lead; he looked at her, sucked his teeth, twisted his little mouth to one side, and gave her that 'I don't know who told you could sing' look. She looked him straight in his eye, wrapped both her little hands around that microphone, took two steps away from the rest of the choir, and begins singing at the top of her lungs.

She let out the sweetest sounds of "Just the other day, I heard a man say that he didn't, he didn't--believe in God's word, but I can say, that the Lord is the way 'cause he's never, never failed me yet". The entire congregation was up on their feet. Someone was shouting "Go on girl; sing the song!"

I remember wanting to laugh when I saw Jarvis face. He was grinning so hard with a brand new 'that's *my* sister' attitude.

Yes, I hope it's those words, "We've come this far by faith", that are giving Jarvis comfort and strength this very moment. I'm thinking mental telepathy; do I believe in it? I don't know, but I sure as hell hope it's working right now. I'm always telling folks to call on the Lord because *he's* PDQ. I repeat to myself HE's PDQ... HE's PDQ. ..

Then I begin saying out loud. ..almost yelling.

Happy moments

Every moment

Painful moments

Difficult moments

Quiet moments...

Right now I'm thinking I want PDQ to stand for the "Nestle Quick" meaning that someone told me a long time ago meant "Pretty Damn Quick!"

I hear the doorknob turn, and stare at the door as it slowly opens. My mind drifts and it dawns on me, Arizona-- How will I get there? I have no money to fly, much less gas money to drive from Texas to Arizona. Again, I'm fighting to hold back tears, I can't think.

Even though I watched the Senator's Chief of Staff come through the door, she still appeared like an angel. Sitting on my desk, her soft-spoken voice said, "I'm so sorry".

"*jMarie*, we've made arrangements for you to take the next flight from Austin to Tucson. It leaves in an hour and twenty minutes. Can you get ready that quick?

"Yes, um, sure" I say shaking my head and trying to hold back my next river of tears.

"But I don't have money to take a flight home. I'll need to…"

"Don't worry; it has all been taken care of."

"But I"

"*jMarie*, listen, Clint will take you home so you can pack. Then he'll get you to the airport. You'll arrive in Arizona at 12:40 in the morning."

Biting my bottom lip to fight back the flood of tears waiting to flow, I put my arms around her and say, "Thank you, oh God, thank you so much".

I'm so embarrassed because one, I had to confess to a co-worker that I didn't have enough money to purchase a plane ticket and two I'm blowing my office image of Ms. Happy-Go- Lucky as I stand here like a baby holding on to a grown woman and crying. I hate they're seeing me this way. I'm so used to being strong. I turn to my desk with my head down, and I try to busy myself. Picking up a stack of papers and a pile of invoices I move them to the other side of the desk and then put them right back where I first started. It's obvious that I'm not thinking straight enough to clean off my desk. She must have been thinking the same thing. Taking the stack of paper from my hands, she lays it on the desk, picks up my keys and tells me "Leave this. We will handle these. It will be okay. Take your keys, get your purse and get out of here. You don't want to miss your flight."

Relieved, and not knowing why I said it, I apologized.

"I'm sorry, I just"… "I just"

"No need for any apologies just be sure to call us on the 800 number and let us know how things are. Don't worry about anything here. We will take care of the office; you just take care of you and your son."

"Thank you" I say and take a deep breath. Yes, I finally breathed.

"Thank you so much."

I live only eight minutes from the office, but today that was the longest drive home.

~~~~

Sitting at the Las Vegas airport, my mind kept wandering to the hospital room and I couldn't stand the pressure building up in my mind; so I decide my luck couldn't get any worst and I wandered over to the slot machines and begin dropping a few nickels in hopes to relieve the enormous stress load I was carrying. The very first nickel I drop in the machine causes bells and whistles to go off and the machine starts dropping what seems like thousands of nickels. The lady next to me says, "Oh my goodness, you are so lucky!" I just got off that machine.

The loud speaker is cracking so bad, I can hardly understand the announcer.

"Now bor – flight, crackling sounds — eight, more crackles, six, flight to Arizona."

"Now boarding at gate number – crackling sounds --, 't son."

"Did they say Tucson?"

"Yes ma'am, they did. They said 816. Is that your flight?"

"Yes it is, and guess what? Today really is your lucky day because you can have all those nickels"

"Really! Are you serious lady?"

"Yes, I'm serious. To be honest with you, I am not so lucky today"

"Oh you are. I had been playing the machine over four hours and didn't win that much."

"Well, now you have won. Do you have kids?"

"Yes, two daughters."

"Well please take those winnings and treat them to something special."

"Thank you Miss, Thank you so much."

"No problem. Enjoy!"

~~~~

The plane lands in Tucson, and all of a sudden, I am scared to get out of my seat, afraid of what I will see or won't see when I get to the hospital. Even though I'm flying first class, I should have been one of the first to get off the plane. But this sudden twisting and turning in my gut has me just sitting here.

"Ma'am, are you okay?"

"Ah, yes"

"You may get off the plane before the other passengers. Are you ready?"

"Actually, I'm not. I think I'm going to throw up; do you have a bag?"

"Yes, one moment."

It was too late; I had thrown up all over myself and the airline flight attendant.

~~~~

My sister Aliza and my father meet me in the emergency room of the hospital. By the looks on their faces, I thought I had already lost my son. I looked at them both and refused to ask the question.

A brief walk down the empty hallway had my stomach all set and ready to give an instant replay of both the office and the airplane scene. As I was walking, a strange feeling came over me. I just started to run to my son's room, not even knowing which room he was in. My sister caught up with me and entered the room before me.

There were cops stationed outside the door. As we entered the room, I couldn't even see the bed because it was surrounded with doctors, nurses, machines and tubes of stuff.

I pushed passed everyone. My heart sunk and again I wasn't breathing,

"Jarvis"

"Jarvis"

He looked at me through the bloody bandages all around his neck and head. He smiled and his head fell limply to the side. My heart melted, and then he closed his eyes.

I gasped and reached out to him. The nurse put her arm around me and whispered, "Since his arrival this is the first time he closed his eyes. Let him get some sleep and we can go to the family lounge and talk."

I exhaled, caught my breath, and exhaled again.

Stretching my neck back as far as I could, I closed my eyes and mouthed the words "Thank you. Thank you, thank you Lord.

I'm sitting here trying my best to focus on all the information the doctor is giving me. I can't even stay focused; I knew I would ask my daughter later, what did this mean and what does that mean? Truly later, was going to have to be tomorrow, because the information overload had my heart exploding and my mind blank.

The doctor started explaining that the gunshot wound to Jarvis neck had damaged his carotid artery and jugular vein and has produced a spinal lesion the same as actor Christopher Reeves.

"Why are you comparing my son's injury to Christopher Reeves; he's not paralyzed."

"Ma'am the injury is at a C6 level."

"I don't…"

Being a doctor's assistant Nikita must have sensed my feeling. She took my arm and said, "Mom, I'll explain it to you later; let's go get some coffee, besides I need a cigarette."

"Nikita I'm going to have to move back to Arizona. Jarvis will need me here until he gets better."

"Thanks mom and I will need you too."

Spotting the security guard, Nikita ask him where they can get a cup of coffee.

He tells them to make a quick left and continue down the hall and go across the courtyard where they will find free coffee and some vending machines.

The guard's heart went out to them as he watched them walking down the hall. He knew who they were; it was all over the hospital that their son/brother was in the same condition as the actor Christopher Reeves.

Arm in arm Nikita and *jMarie* mindlessly stroll down the cold, lonely hallway to the awaiting vending machines. As they approach the vending machines they both were thinking; they don't want to eat; they just want a moment away from the reality. Or, a moment for a reality check, either way, even the vending machines knew they weren't there to eat but to mindlessly stare at its contents.

Test-a-lie or Testify

...listening to testimonies of folks I don't know.

The alarm goes off; I roll over, hit it once, pull the covers up off the floor, tuck them under my chin, and decide that the only church I feel like attending this morning is 'Bedside Baptist'. I had been up almost three days in a row. Deep in my heart, I knew I needed to be somewhere where folks could pray for me, because I just was not about having a relationship with the Lord today. Every time I would think about my son lying there, and knowing that he would never walk again I wanted the Lord to come along and make him well. At the same time, the Lord is the last person I want to talk to. Over and Over I keep asking, "Why? Why, my son?"

I believe that through God all things are possible, so why wasn't it possible that this bullet didn't miss my son?

Right or wrong, I felt that God could have prevented this. Right or wrong, I sure am angry with him today.

Aliza is going through my suitcase; she hasn't bothered to ask was it okay.

"Oh sis, where'd you get this? Oh, I like this."

"Do you mind? I'm trying to sleep, and besides get out of my suitcase."

"Girl, I'm preaching today. I need something different to wear."

"Besides, it will do you good to get up and come hear me preach. Not to mention I could, and would like your support."

I'm thinking my support. Hell, I don't even have support for myself, much less for anyone whose name isn't Jarvis Todd.

And wanna-be Christians are not…

Aliza repeats. "Want to be Christians?."

"Yes, the ones who want to assume the title but not follow the rules."

"Oh those ones."

"Yes those ones. They certainly are not at the top of my list for company today."

Okay, Aliza says as she continues pulling clothes from *jMarie*'s suitcase.

"Oh! This looks nice, maybe I'll wear this"

"Maybe you won't wear anything. Maybe you'll preach naked like Moses did. Or was it Joseph? Or, whoever it was. "If you don't get out of my suitcase you might not have hands to pull some clothes on."

"Girl, stop being so mean. It makes you look like this old timey picture with you and your cousins.

She laughs and puts the dusty as hell photo in my face.

"Look, look at you."

"Girl, if you don't get that dirty, dusty, ugly picture out of my face"

"Here You need a laugh. Look at you, and look at that lovely hair do, and the plaid dress. Ohhh girl!"

"Stop it Aliza. I'm not playing with you."

~~~~

Well two hours later, because it was obvious that Aliza was not going to let me get any more sleep. Here I am, listening to testimonies of folks I don't know. I'm not ashamed to say, right now, I don't even care to know them nor their problems.

I watch Sister Green, as she places both hands on the pew in front of her and pulls up her big 300 pound frame or is it 400 pounds?

She has on the biggest, greenest hat with purple feathers all around it. Her dress is clinging to her. Whatever possessed her to reach back pull her dress, and then fan it, is beyond me. When she did that, the children sitting just two pews behind her went into hysterics. Despite the laughter of the children, and the commotion to remove them from the service, Sister Green never turned around. She plunged right in with the formalities of addressing the pastor.

"To the great pastor of this..."

Suddenly my thoughts began wandering. Just how many years ago was it when some man, somewhere, decided that at his church, all the folks would stand and address his presence right along with addressing the Lord. I think that the only person who needs to be addressed so formally is the Lord, cause, the rest of the folks, including the preacher, should all be equal to folks who want to follow Jesus. Maybe I got more to learn and need to read more scriptures, but today this is how I feel.

I nudge Aliza with my elbow. "See, Sis Green is a prime example of what I was talking about this morning.

"What- a want to be?"

"That's it, she reminds me of a wanna be Christian."

"Aliza, remind me to let you borrow the book a friend of mine sent me.

"What's it about?"

"It's a draft of his book "God is not a Christian" by Carlton Pearson. The title is causing quite an uproar."

"I already don't like the title sis."

"That was my first reaction too but I have to say I agree with him, because we are the ones who are "supposed" to be the Christians. To have the title, we must be *following* God.

Anyhow, the pastor looks at Sister Green, clears his throat, adjusts his tie, and says "Thank you, Bless you," and then nods his head in approval, which only encourages her to continue.

Accepting his cue, Sister Green continues, with a voice loud enough to wake the dead.

"It's an honor to be in the house of the Lord, and to the great pastor of this church and congregation, I just wanted to stand to say, "God is good all the time."

And of course, the congregation, who all know this line, responds with

"All the time; God is good"

"Oh yes!" shouts Sister Green

"All the time"

And immediately, my thoughts are, 'Yeah, well he must have been on daylight savings time when they shot my son.'

I'm half listening to Sister Green as she goes on and on about something or other. Then I lean over and say to my sister,

"I don't know why ya'll insist on letting her get up right before church starts so that she can test-a-lie."

"Did you say test a lie?"

Leaning her head and shoulder slightly to the right, looking at Aliza with a half grin on her face.

"Oops did I say test-a-lie? Girl you know I meant testify!

Shaking her head Aliza looks at her sister "Satan is so busy, test-a-lie?, ump ump, ump, ya know I'm going to have to use that in my next sermon."

"Hey, go on and use it. It certainly will be one of those sermons you can say you had them all on their feet." Matter of fact I hope that's what you will be preaching about when I join your church."

"When you join, you're already a member."

"No, I joined another church when I moved; don't I have to rejoin yours?"

"Ok, sis, you can join again."

"On second thought Aliza, I don't know if I want to rejoin. Let me ask you; when your members' start' *test-a-lying* and testifying do you preach about the fact if they pray more at home they will be able to keep their business between them and the Lord?"

"*jMarie* you know it's good to testify, because it lets others know what God can and has done for you.

"Testify…yes Aliza, but Test- a- lie and getting up in church every Sunday telling everyone all your crazy business…I don't think that's what God had in mind."

"Like I said earlier, it can be good to let others…"

"Aliza, I'm interrupting you because too many times I set in church and wanted to yell out…hey you carry-- your craziness to the Lord in prayer, not in here."

"Well, *jMarie* you can join tomorrow, that's what I'll be preaching about."

"Ooh sis, don't tell me now you are test-a-lying."

"No, I will be preaching about testifying; and I like that --you carry- your crazy-- I think I'll title the sermon YC2."

"Why see to?"

"Yes, as in You Carry, Your Crazy."

Then we both, without even opening our mouths, burst out laughing. With the backs of our hands covering our mouths, we both looked back to see if the usher was back at the door, or coming to remove us from the service like she did the kids earlier.

Suddenly, I realize, this is the first time I have laughed since Jarvis' accident. I close my eyes and let the Lord know I am grateful for my sister insisting that I come to church with her. I have to admit, she does look good in my purple suede suit.

I also let the Lord know that even though I'm upset with him I do know without a doubt, he's the one and only who has taken my hand and led me through some other fires. He is the one I can trust to bring me through this tragedy with Jarvis. I close my eyes and I ask for his forgiveness for my doubting him again.

"*jMarie*, are you daydreaming again?"

"Ah, no, I was just thinking about the time when I was about twelve

I was walking home from school alone. I had turned down the wrong street and was lost. I was crying and when I looked up, I remember standing in front of an old warehouse. Someone had painted in big black letters over the door, "Christians aren't perfect, just forgiven."

"And those words are so true."

"I never forgot them."

"Keep them in your heart, and shh, keep quite because the usher is coming." Whispers Aliza.

The usher reaches our pew. She bends down to whisper something in Aliza's ear. Aliza nudges me as she gets up and follows the usher to the front of the church so she can sit with the other preachers.

Trust me, I am thinking, this could be my easy escape.

Two minutes later, my phone vibrates. Picking it up I read a text from Aliza.

"Don't 'U' leave and remember, Christians are 4given cuz they know G2R."

I smile because she read my mind about leaving. Before I could even put my phone away, it vibrates again -- G2R means Genesis to Revelations. What mom and dad taught us growing up so we would know who to call on in times like these. 45888.

Seeing my code '45888' for -I luv u- made my heart smile. It made me think about the day I came up with the code for when Nikita and Jarvis were out. The promise was to text me to let me know they were all right. The letters on the phone equaled 45888. It became our favorite code.

Smiling I put the phone away and tried to focus on the Mistress of ceremony.

Aliza doesn't really preach she teaches with a sense of humor. I'm sure I can learn something today. I cross my legs, get comfortable and decide to stay and hear her preach.

The humble introduction of my sister, who has many college degrees and accomplishments, made me proud to be her sister. When the Mistress of Ceremonies started off by saying that when she requested Aliza send her bio and introduction statement, my sister told her to simply say, "I am the ordinary, trying to serve the extraordinary."

That simple statement automatically gave Aliza a standing ovation. She put the congregation at ease by saying she was one of them, just an ordinary person. The fancy formalities of addressing her as Reverend, Pastor, Bishop or whatever, was not even necessary.

No sooner had they sat down, they sprung back to their feet with shouts of "Amen," "go ahead sister preach that," "hallelujah," and more.

Then Aliza came down from the pulpit and as she walked down the aisles she said "we need to learn to stop Fellow-whipping and do more Fellowshipping!" She said when we drop the "S" we drop the salvation, the soul, the spirit .and the Savior.

I say to myself, she is right, because I've been guilty of gossiping when I've drop the "s" and start whipping instead of "fellowshipping."

I make a mental note to myself --New Year's resolution; join Aliza's church, again.

~~~~

Try a Like*it*!

...diet, the first three letters are hazardous to your life

It's been four months since Jarvis was moved from the hospital and placed in a nursing home. I rented a small condo in Tucson not far from the nursing home.

Just as I finish checking my emails the phone rings. Caller ID shows it's Aliza so I pick it up.

Hey Aliza, what's up?

"Oh nothing, I'm standing in front of this mirror and asking myself why I don't take this full-length mirror out of my bathroom.

"What are you talking about?"

"I'm talking about looking at my 5 foot 2 inch full figured body completely naked is just not a pretty picture. Oops sorry sis, 't-m-i.'"

"Aliza, full-figure...please, that title belongs to me, and may I add "proudly" belongs to me."

"Ok, *jMarie* I let you have it."

We both start laughing.

"Aliza, what is tmi?"

"Sorry sis, it means too much info. I keep forgetting your tex lingo is limited."

"You mean your new way to talk but *not* talk"

"Not just my way is, it's the new age way."

"Okay, whatever you say, but you can add a "w" as in way-too-much-info."

"Anyhow, back to why I am thinking about taking this mirror out of my bathroom. Last time when I went to visit Jarvis I had on the T shirt you made me."

"Which one?"

"My favorite one, 'Diet' the first three letters are hazardous to your health'

"Oh yeah, the 'Try a like*it*--eat what you like! only ½ of it."

"You know I could be rich, every time I wear the shirt someone wants to buy it right off my back."

"Give out my number, I'll make 'em one."

"Your son, my nephew, is probably the only person who looked at my shirt and said something negative."

"What do mean? Jarvis knows I made that t-shirt, he likes it."

"Well I was about to leave, and you know Jarvis, you have to pray before leaving."

"Hey you're the preacher you know he's going to make you pray."

"He knows I wouldn't leave without praying, but I'm telling you, I almost did that day."

"Why?"

"Well, he read my tee shirt out loud and then said to me; auntie how's that working for you?"

"I told him, not too good, and he said "is that because you're still eating the whole thing."

"Tell me my son didn't say that."

"Not only did Jarvis say it, Lydia was giving him his meds at that time and he started laughing so hard he almost choked on his meds."

"Yes, your son said those exact words sis."

"Girl, Jarvis was probably having a bad day; you know how he's likely to say anything when he's upset."

"You're right sis, but he was having a good day, I had brought him some crab legs and we were laughing about something he was telling me about one of the nurses who did something stupid the other day. We even talked about possibly having the ambulance service bring him to church next week."

"Speaking of Jarvis, I'm glad you called, do you want to go with me tomorrow and see him."

"No, I'm leaving tonight; I'll be out of town for the next couple weeks."

"Oh, ok."

"You know when I was driving home from the visit, I thought about what he said about the shirt not working for me. I call right away and got me a membership to G-I-T"

"G-I-T, What is that?"

"It's the new kickboxing center, Get It Tight." I want to get back to wearing my short skirts like I did when I weighed 102 pounds. Because you know with that number now going from back to front at an even 201 pounds, I can't even be wearing my short skirts."

"Girl you can't be wearing those little short skirts anyhow, you are a preacher now."

"Sis, I did not say "little" short skirts. Besides, I agree with Bishop T.D. Jakes, he said since he has been preaching he has heard about more, long-down to the floor- ruffled skirts coming off quicker than the short ones. He said stop judging. Stop judging!

"Hey sis, I'm not judging…but I hear ya, as for me, I'm getting older now and just want to drop enough weight so I can walk a flight of stairs without getting out of breath. You do the kickboxing thing and since I've lost 49 pounds this year, I'll stick with my like*it*."

I prefer to let folks continue to second-guess what size I really am. I will keep wearing my long tops and throw a vest over it. Because I believe in that old commercial, 'never ever, let them see you sweat' and I like to add, nor count your rolls.'

"*jMarie* stop making me laugh, I'm trying to put my makeup on while talking to you."

"Seriously Aliza, I'm happy that I'm pass the age where I worry about hearing someone say, "She has such a pretty face, but…""

"And you know what they're really thinking is you're pretty, but your fat butt needs to lose some weight."

"Umm, yep that's what I was going to say."

"Hey girl I gotta go, talk to ya later."

"Okay, get yourself a bottle of water and toast to 'Get It Tight'

"Will do…chat with ya."

"Bye sis."

Guarding Your Heart

...taking care of my heart was my job

Hey sis have you had lunch yet?

"No, I was just about to take Jarvis some tacos because I won't see him this evening since Vince and I are going to dinner tonight"

"Don't get the tacos, pick me up on your way to the nursing home and I'll bring lunch for you and Jarvis."

"Oh, I thought you weren't getting back until next week."

"It's been three weeks, I got back last night."

"What did you fry up?"

"I didn't fry up anything, thank you!" since I have been going to 'G-I-T', I have been baking everything. Besides, I want my nephew to see how much weight I lost these past few weeks."

"Aliza come on now...it's only been two, I mean three weeks."

"I know sis, but honestly you can already see it in my face."

"Well Jarvis was just asking if you were upset with him because of what he said about your t-shirt"

"Jarvis knows I don't get upset about stuff like that, did you tell him his comment was a good thing because I've been kickboxing?"

"'j Marie wait, back up did you say you were going to dinner with Vince?"

"Yeah, we've been talking."

"So you're back on again."

"I don't know if back on is what I call it, but ..."

"Sis, I like Vince, he's a nice guy, but honestly he reminds me of my ex, they want to be loved but they are afraid to love."

"Excuse me."

"I'm just saying sis, the two of you are a cute couple, and you need to find out what he's afraid of."

"What makes you think it's him?"

"Because we all know you have a big bleeding heart and you are not afraid of love."

"Truth is we both been hurt and are just taking it slow."

"Slow, j Marie if you let him take it any slower you will be at a stop sign."

"Ha ha Aliza, we are finished with this conversation, I'm on my way out the door now, so be ready I'll be there in fifteen minutes."

"Ok, bye."

"Bye."

Aliza's comment about "find out what Vince is afraid of" made me realize that may be exactly what I need to do. I remember when Vince walked into an event I was at, I had to tell my heart to slow down. There was something about his quiet friendly manner that made me want to know more about him.

But somewhere between my question to him "Are you available?" and his response "You know that I am," I think my heart and reality got crossed.

I remember how pleasantly surprised I was to receive a Valentines card from Vince. I called his office to thank him for the card and invite him to stop by after work and enjoy one of those heart shaped pizzas with me. His response was " I'm working late but we can create our own heart day later on." My dining room table must have stayed set for months with its heart shape plates, white linen napkins trimmed with tiny hearts and the matching champagne glasses.

Despite what Aliza's says, I am excited about my date night tonight. Vince and I always have a good time when we're together.

These past months I've been so busy enjoying the moments with Vince that I probably missed the heart day he had in mind.. (L.O.L) or should it be (LAM) laughing at me. Either way, the funny thing is since I've learn to enjoy the moments it doesn't hurt (as much) anymore.

Pulling up in front of Aliza's house, I blow the horn. My phone goes off and it's Aliza texting 'b*r*t' (be right there).

The time it took her to text she could of grabbed her keys and came to the car.

Aliza comes running out the house with her cell phone glued to her ear.

"Aliza, why don't you get the gadget for your ear so you don't have to keep your shoulder smashed into your ear constantly?"

"Sis it's called a Bluetooth, I can't afford one."

"Stop buying all those workout clothes and I bet you could afford one."

Even though she's calling herself whispering, I heard Aliza when she said "Oh no, not tonight girl, she has a date with Vince tonight."

"Who are you telling my business to now?"

"It's Lydia, she is the nurse on duty with Jarvis, and he told her you were coming by. She wants to know if we want to catch a movie after our visit."

"Aliza, get in the car!"

"So sis, dating Vince again?"

"Yes and like I said on the phone , we are finished with this conversation, let's leave it at that."

"Didn't you tell me he had asked you to take care of him, and you said you told him only if he took care of your heart?"

"Aliza, I'm not having this conversation with you."

"Sis, I'm just saying you've been separated for a while, I won't exactly call that a good job of taking care of your heart."

"Aliza, drop it, besides that was a stupid request on my part. Taking care of my heart was my job not his."

"Oh, well good thing you kept your table set up with the little heart place settings, now you are ready for love day."

"Not love day, it was set for heart day."

"Heart day, love day, Vince day"

"Should I tell him it's been waiting for him?"

"Aliza, what you should do is - mind your business."

"Ok, sis, sorry, just don't want to see you get hurt again."

"I'm a big girl, it will be okay."

"What is on that plate for Jarvis? I hope it's not one of your 'fried what-ever fits in the pan' recipes."

"I told you I'm baking everything now, he'll love it; I learned how to bake the catfish using cornflakes to make it nice and crispy without using oil or flour. I also baked him a sweet potato."

"It does smell good."

"None for you sis, remember its date night."

"Ha, ha, you're funny besides let it go will you."

"Sis, Vince still gets high points for your Tiffany bracelet; I know what you're gonna say, he could have got it from Target and you still would have loved it."

"You're right Aliza, I still would love it, and once again lets change the subject."

"Ok, before I forget do you want to join the GIT club?"

"I told you, I'm sticking with my Like*it*."

"But I can get you in for half price."

"No thanks."

I remember how surprised and excited I was last year when we returned to Vince's house from a very nice birthday dinner and he said, "That's your gift on the table." I had spotted the little turquoise blue bag as soon as we arrived at the house.

"But I can get you in for just half... are you listening to me?"

"What?"

"I said half price!"

"Sorry, you mentioned my Tiffany bracelet, and I was just thinking."

"I thought we were off the topic of Vince."

"We are -- you're the one that mentioned my birthday present."

"Well now I'm mentioning GIT, I think you would like kickboxing."

"It's not for me, thanks. Did I tell you when I got the bracelet from Vince; I jokingly said 'oh, you went to "Jared's'. Vince said, "No, sweetheart, I went passed "Jared's"

"Yes sis, you did tell me that. Are we off the topic of Vince or not?

I guess he'll always hold that special, correction, that very special place in your heart huh sis."

"You are right, he always will."

"Um sis, did Jarvis moved to a new nursing home?"

"What? No."

"Well then I'll need you to focus, because you just missed your turn."

"Oh, crap!"

"And I'll need you to get Vince off the brain."

"Ha ha…you are just full of the jokes today Aliza."

"There's a handicap spot."

"I don't use them unless I have Jarvis with me."

"But your brain is stuck on Vince that makes you handicapped, besides I don't see anything else close."

"Still we can't just take the spot… Pastor Aliza."

"Hey I'm just saying it was close."

"Yeah right."

Brunch

here's to Vince, we know this would have been your breakfast but....

---

jMarie decided to fix a nice brunch for her friend Lydia and her sister Aliza. Nikita said she would stop by if she was in the area.

With the lid in her hand, Aliza prepares her thumb and forefinger to pinch a taste of the fried sweet potatoes and onions.

"Umm sis, you know you hurt yourself on these potatoes."

"And who nominated you as taste tester?"

"Nikita's' not here, so I thought I beat her to the taste testing task."

"Speaking of my daughter, I talked to her earlier and she said she would be a little late. So that probably means we will be finished eating and heading out the door when she arrives."

"Lydia are the mimosas' ready?"

"Yep, just a little more orange juice and they are ready."

"Great I'll have one."

"I'm fixing one for everyone so we can have a toast."

"Aliza get out of the potatoes and come give us a toast."

"Ok…Here's to Vince, wherever you are, we know this would have been your breakfast so we thank you because it is our brunch".

Laughing, Aliza and Lydia shout, "Hallelujah goes right there!"

Shaking my head with a frozen half frown half smile, I glare at them and mutter, "Keep it up you two and it will be your last brunch."

"We're sorry."

"We ain't mad at you girl; you've come a long way, even though Aliza tells me you're dating Vince again."

"Aliza has a big mouth."

"Hey sis, blame it on the preacher in me, I gotta always be talkin'."

"Maybe, but not about my business; unless you're praying for me; and you know I'm picky about who I ask to pray for me."

Lydia pouring her second mimosa says, "*jMarie* I'm with you on that one. Because I know everyone is not praying for my best interest. And don't ever ask sister Noall to pray for you."

Aliza reaches in her purse and pulls out her phone. "This is why my favorite download is the **B-I-B-L-E**. your **B**asic **I**nstructions **B**efore **L**eaving **E**arth."

"Sis you have the Bible in your phone?"

"I have to keep it close; you never know when I might have to text a scripture to someone."

"Hey ya'll I just poured me a second glass of mimosa not communion; don't get me wrong I'll be at church on Sunday morning but right now can we get back to the topic?"

"Lydia you can be such a heathen sometimes, what was the topic?"

"The topic was about you and Vince. When ya'll gonna get married?"

"Lydia you didn't hear a soul mention the 'm' word."

"Hey sis, speaking of the 'm' word, you are lucky. You been married, what--not once but twice, and some of us haven't even been engaged."

"Don't blame me because you are looking for 'quote' Mr. Perfect."

"Hey Lydia, Jarvis tells me you've been checkin' out one of the doctors at the nursing home. He said you asked Aliza to pray for a husband for you?"

"No! That was your son Jarvis being funny one day. Aliza was praying when the doctor came in. Jarvis interrupted her and told her to pray for a husband for me and the doctor said he was available.

Jarvis had a good laugh now he's trying to marry me off."

"Ok, enough of this conversation the food's getting cold.

"Besides how many times do I have to tell ya'll being married is not always all that great, or as the old folks say 'ain't all it's cracked up to be' if you are not married to the right person."

"There you go sis, always trying to drop us a little knowledge. Lydia, how many times you been married?"

"None, I had two proposals, one brotha and a white guy. I am embarrassed to say you could put them together and you wouldn't even come up with half a man."

"Lydia you never told me you dated a white guy."

"Hey it was back in the day, and I was going for Jessie Jackson's rainbow coalition."

"Aliza, she is not lying, Lydia liked 'em all, white, brown, polka dots. She was not discriminating."

Adding the cheese to the softly scrambled eggs, *jMarie* tells the ladies to have a seat."

"Are we going to wait on Nikita?" ask Lydia with her hand

already on the plate of banana walnut pancakes.

"No, we are going to eat our food while it's hot."

Taking her seat and placing the nice hot dish of fluffy scrambled eggs on the table *jMarie* asked Aliza to bless the food.

"Sure, but please tell me those are egg beaters and not whole eggs."

Shaking her head Lydia asked. "Aliza, what do you think they use for the egg beaters?"

"Not the whole egg."

"Don't worry sis, I did use egg beaters because I wanted to get my extra calories from the Velveeta cheese not the eggs; now will you please say the blessings."

"Lord, thank you for this lovely brunch and please let *jMarie* make more dinners for us even though she is seeing Vince again."

"I'm with you Aliza," says Lydia under her breath.

"Aliza, Lydia we are blessing the food, say amen."

"In the name of Jesus, Amen."

"Amen" repeats Lydia as she is reaching for the strawberry jam.

jMarie says, "Back to the topic of men; you two are a trip. Must I remind you that life actually got better for me without a husband, especially when I learned to decrease my expectations."

"Decrease your expectations?" Lydia ponders aloud.

"Yes decrease; my expectations not my self esteem. I learn to not expect my happiness to be bound by a piece of paper nor a man."

"Hey sis, did you ever tell Lydia about the water balloons your first husband left in the car after your honeymoon?"

"No Aliza, can we enjoy our meal and change the topic?"

"Oh I want to hear this. Sounds like you been keeping secrets from me," Says Lydia.

"No, I've been keeping my business to myself"

"You and Lydia been friends for how long and you haven't told her?"

"Go ahead sis, tell her."

"It is not a conversation for the dinner table."

"Girl, this is the brunch table and my stomach can handle anything." Says Lydia as she reaches for the bottle of champagne.

"Ok." *jMarie* begin, "Well my first husband, the day after we returned from our honeymoon, which I paid for. I'm headed to the mall with my cousins. My older cousin was driving because I didn't have a license."

"You didn't have a license, how old were you?"

"Lydia! why do you need every detail?"

"Hey, I just wondered how old you were since you were already married."

"I was twenty when I got married. However, I was twenty-seven before I got my driver's license."

"Twenty seven!"

"I told ya'll, I hate driving. Anyhow, we were driving his car down the road and I reached in the backseat to get my purse. I spotted one of those little water balloons on the floor and I said to my cousin, 'I don't know why he always has these damn water balloons in the car.'

She said, What? Water balloons, for what?"

I said "I don't know. See? and I dangled one in front of her face. She was so mad she let go of the steering wheel and the car veered off the side of the road. She said 'I oughta slap you!' Mind you I was completely confused as to why she wanted to slap me. I said, 'Why? I didn't have 'em, he did.'

And she said. "That's no damn water balloon"

I said 'Yes it is.'

Then she told me 'You are so stupid, *jMarie*, I can't believe you don't know what that is.'

By then I was just dumbfounded. At the time, I really did not know why she wanted to slap me and why she didn't know it was a balloon.

Lydia yells out "girl, don't tell me it was a condom!"

"Yell it to the whole world why don't you. See this is why I haven't repeated the story. I don't need everyone thinking I was stupid when I was younger. Can we eat and just forget this conversation."

"No, no, no, go ahead finish telling us what you did."

"Tell her, not just a rubber, but a used rubber, I mean condom." Aliza chimes in.

"What! Are you serious?"

"Aliza's right, it was used, my cousin was so mad she was yelling, 'you can't be that stupid *jMarie*, you're twenty years old.'

Believe it or not I guess I was. My husband was having affairs and I didn't even know it. Back then I had never seen a rubber before in my life so I really didn't know what it was. Every time I see a balloon to this day; I can still hear my cousin yelling 'I ought to slap you.'"

Lydia interrupts and says "I aint saying I would of killed the nigga, but I would of 'kilt!' the nigga, with a capital K."

"Hey, hey hey!, did ya'll save me some food?"

"Nikita, when did you come in?"

"Mom, I came in just when Ms. Lydia was talking about killing a nigga. Ms. Lydia you must have been rough in your younger days."

"Got that right, I was. Now let your momma finish this story."

"Lydia, I'm not about to finish this in front of my daughter."

"That's okay mom, I'm going outside and have a cigarette, finish the story."

Aliza says 'thank you niece, but you know you don't need that cigarette."

"You're right auntie; I'm going to stop soon so I can start working out with you." Nikita then heads out the door as she lights her cigarette.

With her mimosa in hand, Lydia is on the edge of her chair "Okay jMarie finish the story. Did you really believe him when he told you they were water balloons?"

"Hey I was a newly-wed who had to cut her honeymoon short because I got pregnant on my wedding night."

Lydia sat her glass of mimosa on the table. "On you wedding night? You wouldn't have known that quick girl."

"No, really, I did. Trust me, I knew. The next day I was so sick that we could not, no let me rephrase that, I could not even enjoy myself. My ex-husband had left me lying on the bed bleeding and telling me how stupid and dumb I was, and that it was my parent's fault that I didn't know anything about sex."

"Girl!, no he didn't!. Ump, that explains why you don't be bothered with brothers when they try to rap to you."

"Lydia, will you let her finish her story? Besides, my sis doesn't fall for every brother, because she has Vince. Now let her finish."

"Ok, so I'm crying and apologizing because I didn't know I was on my period."

"Hey girl back then remember we called it monthly or menses." Blurted out Lydia again.

"Whatever it was called. Turned out it was not my period; my cousin had told me later it was because I was a virgin.

"Girl, you should have known Ms. Lydia back then, I could have given you a few tips."

Shaking her head, Aliza says 'Lydia why do we all know that's the truth?' I think I'll start calling you Blanche from the Golden Girls "

"Do ya'll want me to finish or can I stop here?"

"No girl finish, we won't interrupt anymore."

"We, Lydia speak for yourself; you're the one who wants every detail."

"Anyhow, I guess I was stupid to a degree. However, I thought that when we got married my husband would teach me how to do those things. Silly me! I had to chalk that up to a lesson learned about men."

"Girl, you been through some stuff; I'm talking Lifetime TV stuff."

"Did I mention he liked to fight? Ladies only that is; he was such a bastard."

Lydia interrupts again. "That reminds me, one day at the end of my shift I was sitting with your son and Jarvis was telling me how he remembers when he was little he saw your ex-husband throw you through a window. Is that true?"

"Yep, Jarvis was only about three and I never knew he even saw it. Until one day when my mom called me and said Jarvis told her that, his dad threw me out the window."

"This certainly isn't funny, but the way Jarvis was telling the stories about his dad, he had me and the other nurses cracking up when he said that he refers to his father as the sperm donor."

"He and Nikita used that name for their dad since they were in Junior High. I tried to get them to stop, but they never did."

"So Jarvis wasn't lying when he said his dad was a really mean bastard?"

"Nope, he wasn't lying. I'll never forget, after I was pregnant my ex asked for sex and I told him only if we could do it like we did before we got married."

"How was that?" Aliza asked

"With our clothes on."

Lydia picks up her glass and finishes her drink. Putting the empty glass down so hard it sounds like it cracked.

"No you didn't ask that! You actually said with your clothes on?"

"Yeah, I did, dumb me. Got my ass kicked for that comment. Hell,but the truth is with him that was the only way I enjoyed it, or maybe the better word is liked it"

"Girl, you're tough, but now I understand when you would

always say sex is not on the top of your list of things to do."

"I should had just told him no; because two months later, I was pregnant with Nikita; good thing about it is Jarvis and Nikita are the only two good things my ex ever gave me.

Oh no, wait... there was the time before we got married, he brought me an engagement ring, but his mother took it before he could ever give it to me."

"And you still married him?" said Lydia as she stood up.

"Hey the engagement was in the paper the invitations were out, what can I say."

"You are a better woman than me my friend."

"That and my sister is not as hot as you are Lydia."

"Girl when I was in nursing school I guess I've just had lucky experiences, don't hate a lover."

Finished with her cigarette, in walks Nikita. "Are you done with your story ma?"

"Yes, I'm done. Are you going to eat?"

"Yep, but I'm gonna fix my plate to take home."

"Ms Lydia, this time when I come in the door did I hear you say you were a lover?"

"That's right, if I was ten or fifteen years younger I might have had a chance of hooking up with the wood, as in Tiger."

"You know you are too black for him."

"Lydia is mixed. Tell her girl. You ain't black, your parents are just the opposite of Tiger's, your daddy is white, your mama is black right?."

"No, my mama is Indian and my daddy is black."

"Well I'm here to remind you, white folks say you are as black as that cup of coffee you just poured."

Resting her elbow on the table and flipping her hair off her shoulders Lydia says "Where did you think I got this long, soft and gorgeous hair from?"

Nikita gives her head a quick jerk and starts laughing as she reaches over to run her fingers through Lydia's hair. "I think…you got it at the wig store."

Even Lydia had to laugh as she flipped her hair back one more time and said "don't hate, ya'll just jealous."

jMarie says "you see all those wigs in my closet; you know I am not jealous girl."

"Whatever" says Lydia, "I bet Tiger wish he had him a sista about now, huh Aliza."

"You know that's the truth."

"But wait, he really is mixed." Lydia asked with a puzzled look.

"Ms. Lydia, I know you heard Tiger is mixed, trust me mixed or not you can bet right about now… he is finding out just how much of the mixture is black." Says Nikita giving Lydia that –don't be stupid look.

Aliza looks like she is in deep thought over the conversations, then she blurts out. "Listening to you all makes me think we need to come up with another name besides –mixed- it's just like our President. His mama is 'quote' white. But the whole world calls him black."

"True, but he's one of those blacks that white men love to hate; because they are jealous of him."

"What about the other type of white man that hates to love Obama in front of their friends?" says Aliza

"Hey , I'll take the second type because when they go to the voting booth…they vote 'Yes We Can' as they check the Obama box."

"The problem I have is with the brothers who be hate'n on the smartest, finest President to date"

"There's a close-up on the finest-- I aint gonna lie" says Nikita "Cuz Mr. Clinton looks pretty damn good."

"As I was saying I have a problem with the brothers who don't have enough sense to not be jealous of him."

"Even those whites who are proud of President Obama probably hate their ancestors who made up that crazy ass blood law. Huh ma" says Nikta.

"That's it! shouts Aliza, instead of mixed how about we start using the word bloodlined."

Walking pass her sister *jMarie* gives Aliza the bumped fist. "Bloodlined, that just may work, since they say we are the dominate blood."

"Right sis, it does make sense, because what it actually means is your blood is lined with something else and who knows what.

"Auntie I have to admit it sounds silly but I like it now that you explained it."

"Look I am not sure how we got from my ex-husband, to Tiger Woods blood to President Obama. But ending this conversation talking about my favorite President is a good thing."

"Sis you have lots of food left, do you want me to fix a plate to drop off for Jarvis before going to the movies?"

"Mom you didn't tell me you were going to the movies."

"Nikita, I didn't tell you because you said you had plans for the afternoon."

"You right mom, I forgot that quick."

"Ladies are you sure you don't want to catch a later movie?"

"Lydia, NO! The meter is about to expire on our lovely time together, and tonight I have other plans."

"Oh! My mom uses the meter 'expired' on ya'll too. I thought it was just me."

"Oh yeah, she uses that on us when it's friend day and Vince night."

They all laugh.

"Or how about – I'm outta pocket."

"Oh yeah, sis gives us the outta pocket line to."

jMarie glances at each of them and flips her hand in the air as if to say 'whatever'.

"By the way ladies, about our earlier conversation, we will never have it again, or you will never have my sweet potatoes and onions nor my sweet potato pie ever again-- understood "

"Understood." Aliza and Nikita repeat in sync.

"Got it girl." Says Lydia as she drinks the last drop of champagne from the bottle.

"Good and really I enjoyed your company, thanks for coming over."

"Sis, you sound so white; thanks for coming over."

"Yes mom, that is so white."

"Nikita it's not white, it's proper; which by the way comes in all colors. Get Jarvis' plate so we can go."

Nikita slowly picks up the plate, softly smacks her lips together but loud enough for her mom to hear her, mocking her mom she repeats "thanks for coming over" as she holds the plate gently with her two pinky fingers extended.

"I got Jarvis plate, mom, let's go."

<u>D</u>eserve *what we* <u>T</u>olerate (DTs)

Mother is being moved to a new nursing home tomorrow. All I want to do is get home take a long hot shower and prepare my mind for her move. She said she is excited about it but I really don't think she is.

I get in the house and I am greeted with the light on the answering machine flashing non-stop. I press the play button.

"Mom are you home...mom"

"Get out! Get the f out !"

The words and the tones of the voices coming through my answering machine made me quiver, and I immediately wonder if my 3 year old granddaughter was anywhere near all that confusion. I stop the answering machine and call my daughter.

"Nikita, its mom, what's...?"

"He's mad because I ate corn dogs

"Could you let me finish my question?"

"Oh, sorry mom, I need to get out of this situation as fast as I can."

"As I was asking, what is the problem?"

" When he called me and asked me what I wanted for dinner I told him I had promised Jarvis when I got off work I would bring him a couple of corn dogs. Jarvis wanted me to stay and eat with him so I did."

So I don't know why the hell he went and fixed this damn

chicken a la whatever, and now he's got an attitude because I ate corn dogs."

"I mean seriously Nikita, you guys couldn't find something better to argue about than hot dogs"

"Not hot dogs mom, corn dogs."

"Ok, hot dogs, corn dogs, whatever. Nikita, are you just in an argumentive mood, or what?"

"Mom, why you always take his side?"

"How am I taking his side?"

"I just asked you if…"

"You always take his side; I'm your daughter, not him."

"O…k, you know what, I just got in from spending the day with my mom. I had to clean her room from top to bottom. I swear that nursing home must only clean once a month. I'm tired and all I want to do is get in the shower. Your phone message sounded like you two were about to kill each other, and I was worried about my granddaughter."

"This is as bad as the last time you left me a message about him throwing out your pots and pans because he didn't like the smell of the chitterlings you were cooking."

Of course right now I'm thinking to myself, 'If she had been with a brother she wouldn't be going through all this. He would have called and told her to bring him something home for dinner, instead of home fixing her dinner.' But, that is a whole different ball game.

"You know Nikita; it may be time for you to get out of this relationship"

"Relationship, not quite the word I would choose mom."

"Ok, whatever you want to call it. It's still time for a change. As I say, 'We deserve what we tolerate." The two of you are definitely getting to a point where you don't even appreciate each other because you don't care about each other"

"Yep, you're right mom. I must admit I really don't care for him or his nasty ass attitude anymore."

"Well, do what you have to do Nikita"

"Yeah yeah mom, like you always say, "You can't spell appreciate without using the letters c-a-r-e. Right now, when it comes to him, you can bet care is nowhere near my choice of words. Too bad there's not two ss's now then I could come up with a word."

"You know mom Jarvis and I were just talking about how if it weren't for our kids we both would be looking for new partners.

"What is Jarvis complaining about?"

"Mom, I think he's just tired of everything."

"Jarvis had one of the CNA's call me today because he wanted me to take a blood test to check his levels."

"Is something wrong with his blood?"

"That's just it mom; he wanted to find out if something is wrong, but he said the nurse was being an asshole and wanted to take the blood from his leg."

"Nikita won't that cause him spasmism ?"

"Right mom, that's why he asked them to take it from his foot," He's pissed because the nurse told him he can't feel it anyway so shut up and let them do it where they want."

"Why didn't Jarvis call me, I would of went or called over

there."

"Mom, he called me because he wanted me to come and do it."

"Nikita you know you can't just walk up in there and take his blood."

"Mom, they do so much wrong in there they would have to take me to court and then me and Jarvis will expose them to all the wrong shit they are doing."

"Nikita, I'm sure we can work this out in a calm manner."

"There you go mom thinking they will do the right thing; I guess you are going to do your usual c-i-v *it*."

"Nikita there is nothing wrong with checking it out, investigating and verifying. It just helps when you present the facts."

"That's just it mom, they are a state run facility and they don't give a damn about what your facts are."

"Ok Nikita let's change the subject."

"Oh mom, Jarvis was also complaining about something Raquel did or said today."

"I see his number is on the missed calls, I'll call him back before I lay down."

"Mom thanks for calling and calming me down. I will talk to you tomorrow. Love you."

"Love you too Nikita."

I hang the phone up and push the play button to finish listening to my messages.

"Umm (there's a long pause) mom, just wanted to say hi. Call me back in the morning if you have time."

I could tell there was definitely something wrong with Jarvis, but

I could not pinpoint what. It didn't sound like he was sick but it did sound like something was bothering him real deep, real hard. Guessing from what Nikita just told me sounds like an ulcer named Raquel.

I hang the phone up and call him right away.

"Hey Jarvis, its Mom."

"Hi mom, it's late. You're not sleep?'

"No, actually been on the phone with your sister."

"Ump, I talked to her earlier today. It sounded like they were at war over there."

"I know. She said they were fighting about dinner; let's not even go any further with this conversation."

"Thanks Mom, because I didn't feel like talking about her problems anyway. She chose that silly guy. What do you always tell us? You deserve what you tolerate. Right."

"Right."

"I understand from Nikita your day didn't go so well today; Did you do any water therapy?"

"No, I just wasn't in the mood after that silly ass nurse wanted to take blood from my leg instead of my foot."

"Do you want me to call the doctor and ask him to tell them to use your foot only for the blood?"

"Please do that mom."

"Okay, I'll call first thing tomorrow. What else is the matter?"

"Nothing really. I called to talk to my son today. When Raquel answered the phone she answered "Tim?" and I said "What the... What the hell would he be calling you for? "We got in a big argument and then she said she wasn't bringing my son to see me tomorrow.

"Who is Tim?"

"He's the reason I'm laying here paralyzed"

"What? You know who shot you?"

"Mom, let's not talk about it."

"But you told me you didn't know"

"Mom, I said I don't want to talk about it"

"Ok, sorry."

"How about I pick your son up when I get off work tomorrow and I'll bring him by to see you."

"Would you mom? Thanks."

"No problem son. Get some sleep and we'll see you tomorrow"

"Love you."

"Love you too."

"Goodnight."

I couldn't sleep that night, nor the next two nights, because all I could see was my son lying there wanting to go and choke Raquel and get his kid away from her. I could feel the pain in my heart just as clear as if it was me who could not move and needed to get up and handle some business. I felt his blood pressure rising as I lay in my bed and tried to imagine how it must feel being hurt that bad by someone you once trusted and loved.

Father's Day & Growing Up

…he was loving and teaching; and teaching and loving

Today is Father's Day and I cannot wait to take Jarvis the card I made for him. I promised him I would go by "The Onyx Room" and get some catfish and some of his favorite ribs and have an indoor picnic at the nursing home today.

Stopping by the Hallmark store three times this week, I left crying on all three occasions. It was hard looking through the cards because it seems everyone had a comment about doing something that required some type of limb movement. The last time I gave Jarvis a card about walking he got upset with me. He said I was not being considerate of the fact he was paralyzed.

~~~~

Despite my three trips to the Hallmark store, I had completely forgotten to pick up a card for my dad.

My hair is a mess and I have on the worst pair of sneakers I own. I pray a small prayer that I will not run into anyone I know as I pull into the Walgreens parking lot to get some paper plates and my dads' card.

Since dad is coming to the nursing home today to see Jarvis, I'm praying all the cards haven't been picked over.

Great! The third card I pick up is perfect for dad.

When I get in the car, I search for a pen so I can sign dads' card.

~~~~

Dear Dad,

Just wanted you to know how much I admire, respect and most of all LOVE you, and appreciate all that you and mom have taught me and Aliza.

As I was looking over the cards, it brought back some childhood memories. I remember how I loved to read 1 Corinthians chapter 13. I would read it maybe two or three times and then tell mom that I had read ten chapters. (thinking I got away with it) I now realize that I didn't get away with anything. I guess you and mom knew if I could instill the "LOVE" chapter in my life that I probably would make it through life. For that I say Thank you. I Love you !

jMarie

I lick the envelope and set it on the seat so I won't forget it. I pick up the phone and call dad.

"Hey Dad, it's *jMarie*"

"Hey *jMarie* how are you? What time is the barbeque today?"

"About four o'clock are you coming"

"You bet ya. I'm sitting in one of these cars with the a/c on and cooling off while I eat my light lunch; saving room for the barbeque."

"Ok dad well I just called to say hi! And to remind you about the BBQ…"

"Ribs, potato salad, baked beans, nope I haven't forgotten."

"Ok, I'll see you in a few hours."

The indoor picnic/father's day gathering was really nice. Some of Jarvis friends showed up. They pushed Jarvis bed outside so he could have a 'smoke' and I'm sure it wasn't just cigarettes they smoked with him. When they came back in the room he was very talkative and laughing a lot.

It was such a nice change to see Jarvis laughing and talking so much that I must admit I didn't care at that moment what he had been smoking. It was just good to see him happy. Besides Nikita keeps reminding me that Jarvis is not breaking the law getting high because he has a doctor's prescription for it. I don't understand the legalities of it, so I just finally accepted it.

When I told Jarvis I never smoked he said "Mom you've never had fun, so before I leave this earth I want to get high with my mom's just once."

"Son, I've went all these years not smoking that stuff. I think I can continue without doing so."

"Mom, please --think of it as a last request from your dying son."

"Jarvis… don't make comments like that."

"Mom, it's not like you'll get hurt, besides we would probably just get the munchies and laugh all night long."

He made me promised that one day I would spend the night with him and smoke one joint. Even though I'm scared to try it, it makes me smile to think about it. I keep hoping he forgets I made that promise.

~~~~

I few days after Father's day I went to visit Jarvis, he said he was really tired and didn't want company today. My feelings were hurt so I decided to take a long drive.

Riding down the road I passed an old grocery store all boarded up and the sign swinging from its window was a huge bottle cap Nehi Orange cream soda sign. It brought tears to my eyes as I thought about my father, and I remember it was the Orange Bowl, or some kind of bowl. I guess I always think it was the Orange bowl because I remember my dad went to the store and brought back all these orange cream sodas, root beer sodas, Oreo cookies and ice-cream. He told Aliza and I if we were for the Oreo's team then we could have the Oreo cookies and orange cream soda, and if we were for my mom's team, we could have the Root beer floats. I'm sure there were other times we sat and watched sporting events with my parents but this is the first one that I remember plainly because it was like we were having a big ol party. Oreo cookies, orange cream soda, root beer floats; oh yeah we were partying.

Patting my hand up and down through the mail and papers in the passengers' seat I find my cell phone to call my dad at work.

I hate that my dad still has to work because his Social Security is not enough to cover all his bills and medicine. I got to get my invention licensed so I can help him out.

"Hey dad just checking to see how you're doing after eating all those ribs the other day."

"Oh *jMarie* I'm doing fine. I only ate a couple."

"Ok, dad, it looked like more than a couple to me; and I packed you a dozen to take home."

We both laugh.

"Dad do you need anything?"

"Nope, doing just fine thanks."

"Ok, well I'll see you later, I…"

It was as if he knew I was about to say I love you. He launched right into how family needs to communicate better. He said;

"I was just thinking the other day, whether or not my father ever loved me. Then I thought about how he would allow me to go to his sock drawer and get out baseballs to play with. Thought about how he would give me nickels to go to the store and buy candy and sodas. Then I realized yes, he did love me, as I remembered those days playing with the baseballs, and skipping to the store to spend the money he had given me. Ump--… and the memory gave me a huge relief to suddenly realize, that my father did love me."

I pull the car over to the side of the road to give my dad my complete attention, because I know this is truly a "Hallmark, MGM moment. Not to mention that I can't see the cars in front of me because the tears are rushing down my face and the lump in my heart is so huge right now I'm speechless. Not sure what made him go on and on like this.

Then dad said, "You see my father never said 'I love you' but what I realize now is that those are just words that Hollywood uses mostly as a money maker; they use those words to manipulate and confuse folks from the real meaning of love."

I could hear and almost see the sadness in my dad's voice when he said;

"I can't recall my father ever saying those three words, but I really know now that he did love me his style, his way. And now I know, the only reason he didn't say "I love you" was because his father probably never told him and his father's father never told him so, they never learned how to say I love you, for they had no teacher, no example.

Wiping my eyes and finding a relief in my throat, I wanted dad to know I heard every word. Not quite knowing how to comfort him, I say, "Your dad was a chiropractor, right?"

"Right. He was such a fast runner that he was asked to do speed training at Price University, making him the first black coach at Price. He also played professional football for the old Casino Aggies after WW1"

"Oh I didn't know grandpa played professional football." I didn't know he was the first black coach either. Wow"

"Yep, he sure was. That's information we should get for the grandkids and the great grandkids."

"Did you know your Aunt Betty was training to run in the Olympics, but then the war came and she didn't get to go?"

"Yeah, seems I do remember her telling me and Aliza that."

I'm glad I went this route with the conversation, because now I don't hear that sadness in my dad's voice as he proudly talks about his sister, my favorite aunt.

No matter what happened as I was growing up I remember that me, my sister and my cousins knew we could always go to Aunt Betty's house for good food or just plain ol' comfort.; and Aliza will tell you, sometimes an old fashion spanking. Me, I never got a spanking. Aliza had what my auntie called a 'quick mouth.'

"Well *jMarie*, do you need anything? My lunch time is just about over."

"Oh no dad, just wanted to say ..."

"Okay, well love you."

"I love you too dad."

"Bye."

"Bye."

While my eyes are tearing up I can't even find the end button on my cell phone. Blinking and wiping my eyes, I finally turn the phone off. My mind is so full of happy /sad thoughts it's crazy.

It's as if dad knew I was going to remind him that the last time we spoke I had said "I love you" and he responded with "Ok, bye."

Then I repeated "Dad, did you hear me? I said, I love you".

For the first time since I was away from home did I recall hearing him say back to me "I love you." Back then I could tell they were just words coming from his mouth. I could tell he felt uncomfortable saying it; but I tucked his words deep in my heart. When I hung up the phone, I knew my dad really did love me.

It crept into my mind and thoughts, how I would not have heard those words from my dad that day if I had not said "Dad, did you hear me? I said I loved you."

Now fumbling for my keys to start the car, I look up, close my eyes and I mouth the words "Thank you Jesus". Then I smiled to myself and starting singing in my best voice, "Hallelujah goes right there!

THANK YOU LORD. Thank you for not allowing me to embarrass myself nor my dad by asking him does he love me. Thank you Lord for having my dad share a part of his heart with me. It was as if Dad was finally able to close a chapter in his life at age seventy-six, and was content with the thought that those two simple gestures on his father's part were tucked deep in his heart as the true meaning of love.

Even though I felt like I was on top of the world, I was angry with myself for being so damn selfish all these years and for spending restless days and nights wondering how much my father loved me.

I think back and love couldn't flow any deeper than all the Sunday afternoon rides dad would take us on, or the picnics in the park, or the Saturdays and Sundays he would take us to the school playgrounds and push me, Aliza and my cousins on the swings till we were just about to get sick from so much fun.

Seems like only yesterday I can clearly see my dad's hands as they grip the bars on the merry-go-round and his work shoes all dusty from the dirt, one foot in front of the other as we are yelling "Faster, faster!" and dad kicks up more dirt and gives us the ride of our lives. I remember one time I was trying to get my dad's attention to tell him my cousin was sticking his foot out and dragging it;. My dad said, "Stop tattle -tailing and enjoy the ride." As the dust was flying all around, dad would never tell my cousin to stop. He just kept on running and then he gave us that big final push and we were spinning just like we were on a ride at Disney land.

I remember how I couldn't wait for the last day of school because my dad and my uncles would take us on overnight camping trips with our cousins.

I thought about all those hot summer nights, when dad would make homemade ice cream. He would let us have the dasher so we could lick the ice cream out before it was time to serve.

I thought about all those winters when mom and dad would

wake us to show us it had snowed. Then we would get dressed and go help shovel the walks. Dad would start a snow ball battle with the neighbors. I remember how he would take us skiing, tobogganing, and sledding and how mom always sent a big thermos of her hot chocolate made with can milk and marshmallows. Mom knew all the milk bubbles would be gone but she still used the hand mixer to whip up all those milk bubbles for us. Even though mom had always packed extra pairs of gloves, I remember how sometimes, dad would let us wear his gloves and he would not even have any on. He would turn the car on and let our gloves dry so we could go back out and play.

I'm reminded how my parents taught me how to write out dad's business statements and to always put thank you with a happy face at the bottom of each statement. I remember they taught me how to keep my dad's books, and do taxes.

My list of " how I know my dad loves me" is so overwhelming compared to the two things that my dad just told me his father did that made him feel loved.

I'm reminded of the time that I had decided I was too grown, and I was going to leave home, I had packed my things at the age of seventeen and decided that I wanted some freedom. My father came into my room after I packed and said "Think about this. You're going to break your mothers' heart if you leave."

I remember sitting there crying, but I felt I just had to get away. I had graduated from High School and had a job with the Bank. However, I was not allowed to date, I remember wanting freedom.

I took one last look around my bedroom that day, wiped the

tears from my eyes, picked up my luggage (my graduation gift from my parents).

Cleared my throat, and headed downstairs.

My father was waiting in the car to take me to the YWCA. I remember sitting in the back seat crying all the way there, but thinking how I was going to be so grown and no one could tell me what to do anymore. I would be living on my own and making my own decisions.

I remember how proud I was that I had some money and I was going to be paying for my own room.

My father did not help me get my things out of the car. When I got to the desk at the YWCA, the woman asked

"Are you *jMarie?*"

"Yes ma'am."

"Well, your father has paid for your first week."

"Oh."

"This is your key. If you lose it, you'll have to pay $3 for a new one."

As we walked down the long hall to my room, she belted out the rules:

"No one is allowed in your room.

There is a TV in the main lobby for all girls to watch.

Company is allowed in the main lobby room only."

We must have passed 24 rooms before she said, "This is your room.

The door is unlocked because we just finished prepping the room for you. Your bedroom door must stay locked when you are not here."

l looked around the room. The twin bed was covered with a big, itchy looking tan blanket with black letters YWCA circled in the middle. like it was some nice design.

Already I was homesick. I was missing my old bedroom with the black and white crochet blanket with matching pillows my mother had made me for graduation. I was missing my pajama bag/radio/doll I left behind for my little sister. Growing up we were not allowed to listen to the radio. When I showed Aliza the hidden radio in the pajama bag, she was so excited, she kept putting her finger to her lips saying shhh…and she would point to her ear and give me the biggest grin.

I walked to the nightstand and set the key down next to the black telephone.

Then I had a happy thought "Oh…I can call anybody I want."

My thoughts were quickly interrupted when she said "No phone calls in or out after 9 p.m."

When you hear two short rings and one long ring followed by two more short rings that means you have a phone call because your room number is 212."

I remember not sleeping at all that night. After seventeen years of wanting to have my own room, (that I wouldn't have to share with my sister and my grandmother) that night in my own little private room at the YWCA, I wanted to be back home.

That night I didn't like having my own room. It felt so cold and lonely and my heartbeat between sobs was all I could hear that night. Not only did it break my mothers' heart that night, but it broke mine also. I felt so guilty for causing such grief to my parents that I didn't want to embarrass them any longer. I had to stand up on my two feet and prove that I could be a grown woman. That night I made a vow to not go back home,

Besides, I used to talk about my cousins who left home and then in two months were back at my auntie's. I didn't want folks talking about me that way. I knew I had to prove myself, no matter how much it hurt. So I never went back home; until two kids and a husband later. I don't know which was worse, me taking my husband and two kids back to my parents or my cousins going back and forth to my auntie's all the time.

Okay, I do know which was worst, me bringing all my baggage back to my parents. It just wasn't fair to such great parents, who taught me the meaning of 1 Corinthians 13. And the greatest of these is Love!

I wish that I wasn't driving down the road right now because I wanted to be right next to my dad so I could look him in the face and throw my arms around him, and give him a hug for life. I want to tell him how sorry I am for all the times I was a disobedient child, I want to tell him I'm sorry I didn't appreciated all the love he had given me. I want him to know from the bottom of my heart that I truly love him. After all, people always said I was just like him.

It seemed dad would never say no, and he was always trying to see what he could do to help somebody. If he couldn't do it he was always offering me and Aliza's help. We just didn't have enough sense back then to know that he was loving and teaching and teaching and loving.

Now I appreciate my father in a completely new light and I regret spending so much time on the self pity thinking my father didn't love me.

I'm so choked up that he had such little display of love yet he managed to display so much love. Knowing the truth is he just didn't say I love you because he didn't know how to say it.

If I hadn't been so busy thinking woe is me, I would have been able to realize that my dad's actions spoke way louder than those three words ... 'I Love You'.

Catfish Tacos

"…your taste buds were nominating me as your weekend chef."

"Hey girl. What's up?"

"Ah, I don't know … work!"

"Oh, my bad. Hey we were just talking about having some catfish tacos Saturday."

"We? Who the hell is we?"

"Um, me and Lydia."

"Oh, ya'll decided that your taste buds were nominating me, as your weekend chef?"

"It wasn't like that. I was going through the ads and noticed Corner Market has catfish fillets on sale."

"Hmm, and I'm the only one who knows how to cook catfish?"

"No, but you're the only one who knows how to make catfish tacos."

"Whatever."

"Of course that is if you're not too busy, or should I say, if you're not out-of-pocket."

"You all might be in luck. I may not be out-of-pocket this weekend, since I will definitely be out of pocket next weekend."

"Good, call me back and let me know for sure so I can call Lydia."

"Ok."

"I got work to do, chat with ya later"

"Bye"

~~~~

Now tell me, why does my stomach have the nerve to be growling? I wasn't even thinking 'bout lunch, much less catfish tacos.

I'll never forget the first time I made catfish tacos; it was all a mistake, I had asked the butcher for catfish fillets. When I got home, and unwrapped the fish, I was pissed. It was like he had ripped, not cut, but ripped the fillets into little pieces. I called the store to say I was returning the fish; it wasn't what I had ordered. The butcher said, he thought I had asked for the "catfish on sale" and the only thing on sale that day was "catfish nuggets." I was too far from the store and not about to make a return trip.

So I rinsed the fish in cold water and seasoned it with some lemon and garlic pepper. Then I beat together two eggs with a little water in a small bowl. In a zip-locked baggie, I poured some cornmeal mix with a little bit of "Jiffy" pancake mix to sweeten it up, cause I like everything to have a sweet taste to it. Then I deep-fried the small pieces of fish in my "fry baby." It turned out to be the best catfish I ever had. I happened to have me some gorditas' "sweet" tortillas. I placed a few of the crispy fried nuggets, along with some sour cream, salsa, and avocados on the gorditas. My greedy butt ate about three. No I'm lying, must have been about five. Okay, okay, stop thinking about catfish tacos. You have two more hours before lunch.

Thank goodness, the phone rings taking my mind off food.

I no sooner hang up and there goes the phone again. It has truly been ringing all morning long.

"Hello"

"Hey ma'. You sound so white."

"Hey Jarvis. It's not white, I keep telling you and your sister it's just proper. Anyhow, how are you doing today?"

"Fine mom, can you come by this afternoon and bring me some tacos from Jack in the

"What's with the tacos this week? I just talked to your Aunt Aliza who was begging me to make some catfish tacos."

"Oh, that sounds even better mom"

"Yeah, but I'm not making them until Saturday"

"Oh. Well, will you still pick me up something for lunch today to hold me over till Saturday?'

"Ok. I only have a few minutes. I won't be able to visit long today. I have an appointment at 1:15."

"That's okay Mom. Call when you pull into the side lot of the nursing home. My friend is here, and she'll meet you outside"

"Does she want tacos too?"

"Please mom, bring her one."

"One?"

"Oh, not a taco, she likes the triple meat patty melt"

"Triple? Would it be triple or single if you were paying?"

"Come on mom. Please? She worked all night and then drove for three hours to spend the day with me."

"No problem Jarvis. Does she want fries and a drink?"

"Mom," he says in a low whisper, a can barely hear him.

"She looks like she weighs a ton now. Last thing she needs is fries with the triple meat."

"Jarvis, who is holding the phone for you?"

"One of the workers, my friend went to use the restroom."

"Oh, I hope you don't talk like that when she's there."

"Besides Jarvis, I haven't seen many of your skinny friends going out of their way to visit you."

"Sorry mom, you're right. I should appreciate her more. Thanks for the reminder. Go ahead, add the "super super size fries and drink to her order.""

"What about you?"

"Nah mom, I'll just have the tacos."

"What do you want to drink?"

"I still have some raspberry tea your friend Ms Jeri made for me. That shit is so good."

"Jarvis…"

"Oops, sorry mom, I meant stuff. It is some good tea though."

"Okay. I gotta go. Make sure your phone is on, so I can call when I'm in the parking lot."

"I will. Love you Mom."

"Love you too Jarvis."

A Mothers Love

".. mom, thank you for making up the holiday for me and my sister."

I have not seen Jarvis since I dropped off his tacos three days ago. It has been a long day today, but I need to stop and see him then stop by and see my mom before I go home. I know once I hit my couch, I will not be going back out tonight.

When I arrive at the nursing home, Jarvis wasn't looking so good. I go out to the nurses' station to find out what his day was like.

First shift nurse said that he has been sleeping most of the day and he refused any physical therapy today.

I hate walking in his room and he has all the blinds closed. I know it's been this way all day, not a bit of sunshine in his room.

I open all the blinds.

"Mom, I don't want the blinds open."

"Hey Jarvis. You need some daylight in here; I know they haven't been opened all day"

"Right, they haven't, because I didn't and don't want them opened.

Mom, I've been thinking about Grammy today. When I had the CNA call her, they said she couldn't talk. Have you talked to her today?"

"No son. I am going by to see her when I leave here. I'll call you from her room and let you talk to her."

"Okay, mom. Don't forget."

"I won't."

"Oh, mom, will you bring that picture of you and my Grammy looking real pretty and smiling?"

"You mean the picture from my wedding?"

"Yeah, but not the one with my sperm donor dad in it."

"Not what?"

"My sperm donor dad"

"Jarvis, that's not right, I told you to stop saying that."

"Maybe not Mom, but you know it's true."

We both laugh.

"Sure. I will have to search for it. I just put a lot of those photo boxes in storage, maybe this weekend I can look for it."

"Can't you do it tonight or tomorrow? I really want to put it over there on the night stand; I want to look at my Grammy every day, she said she has me and Nikita's picture by her nightstand."

"Ok, I'll try to find it tomorrow; in the meantime, if I don't find it, can I bring you another picture?"

"As long as my dad's not in it."

"Ok, ok, I got that message; I'll find the one with me and my mom."

"Mom, please don't forget. I want to put the picture by that poem you wrote for Grammy. She said she loves that poem."

"Speaking of the poem, mom will you read it to me, then will you move it over here on the night stand where I'm going to put Grammys picture?"

He moves his head slowly to nod towards the nightstand.

I can see it is painful for him to move his neck.

Reaching up to get the poem off the wall, I hit the side bar on his hospital bed.

"Shit! …Ouch! Mom be careful, Shit."

Apologizing *jMarie* says "I'm sorry son; I was trying to reach the poem"

"There, I got it."

"Read it please."

"Okay."

"Thanks mom, I didn't know you wrote that until Grammy told me the other day. It's really nice. Why don't you have your name on it, so people don't steal it?" Get it protected."

"What's it called?"

"Copyright."

"Yeah, that's it. I bet you could get a lot of money for that poem if you sold it for a Mother's Day card."

"Ump, I never thought about that. You could be right son; I might need to start thinking about it."

"Mom, do you remember when I was little I found your book of poems."

"I sure do because you wrote all over it and crossed my name out."

We both laughed.

The nurse walking by poked her head in the room and asked, "is that Jarvis laughing?"

Lifting his head up slightly, Jarvis says

"It's me girl! What's up, you pulling another shift?"

"Yeah your friend called in sick."

"Again? Ya'll may need to fire her ass."

"Hey man, I'm glad to see your blinds opened; and don't talk like that in front of your mamma."

"My mom's cool. Sorry Mom you know I mean no disrespect."

Hearing Jarvis laughing sounded good.

"I know son, no disrespect taken...your laugh made my heart smile."

"Mom back to your book of poems, I remembered I crossed your name off because I had to do a school project, I used some white shoe polish to white out your name; then I wrote my name on the cover; I'm surprised you remembered."

"Remembered! How could I forget? I was so mad that you messed up my book cover."

"Is it still in that big Bible?"

"Yep, but the Bible is in storage too."

"Mom, you put a Bible in storage! You would have yelled at me and Nikita if we did something like that."

"Son, I moved from a house to a small condo. I still have my other Bible; I just didn't have a lot of room for everything."

"Ma what would you say if I said I didn't have room for an extra Bible?"

"Jarvis let it go; besides it was the one that was all worn out. And you remember I always told you, a Bible worn out is a soul held together."

"Ok, you win mom."

"So, back to my book of poetry you wrote all over."

"Mom, I can't remember, did I spell my name right?"

"Yes son, you did; I'll find it and bring it with the picture tomorrow."

"Really mom? That will be cool.

Sorry, but I'm tired. When you come back tomorrow you can stay longer; and don't forget to bring Grammy's picture."

"Ok, son. I have to stop by Sunshine and see my mom before I head home anyhow."

"Tell Grammy hi and I tried to call her today but they said she wasn't taking calls. Tell her I love her."

"I will son."

Bending over to kiss Jarvis good night, I hit the bed again.

"Oops"

"Damn it mom; will you stop hitting the damn bed."

"I'm sorry; I was trying to be careful. Do you want me to ask the nurse to give you something for pain?"

"No. By the time they decide to bring it, I'll probably be sleep, and I don't want their dumb asses waking me up."

"Son, must you cuss so much?"

"Mom, I keep telling you this is a State run nursing home, they don't give a damn who they hire. Besides, cussing at their asses is all most of them understand before they even do a little something for you."

"Well, maybe it's time we start looking for another nursing home."

"No because I'll just have to go through all the stupid shit again.

Besides, I'm tired of moving,"

"You know son, I've been thinking really hard that maybe it's time I take you home with me, let's talk about that option tomorrow."

"Good night, I love you."

"I love you too mom."

"Mom, the poem you wrote for your mom, it works for you too. Your love never runs out either."

"Ah, thank you son. That's a really nice thing to say, even though I know there are days I don't deserve such praise."

"Yes you do mom; you always do."

"Sleep good son. I love you. Remember, 4 -5- triple 8s."

"And mom, thank you for making up the holiday for me and my sister."

"The holiday?"

"You remember the day after the fourth of July."

"Of course . the I Love my kids day."

"That's it, I always saved some of my fireworks for the next day."

"Jarvis do you remember how you and Nikita tried to eat the whole cake I would make for I Love my kids day."

"No Nikita would try to eat it all not me. Mom, now you're making me hungry for the cake. Will you make one but without the nuts."

"Yes son, maybe this weekend. Goodnight."

"Goodnight mom."

Jarvis must have been thinking about his grandmother all day. As soon as

I get home, I will have to find the picture and my book of poems for him.

~~~~

Leaving Jarvis room, I reach in my purse for my phone so I can call my mom to see if she wants anything before I get there.

"Sunshine Nursing Home"

"Um, yes, room 809 please."

Sorry, the patient is not taking calls tonight."

"Excuse me?"

"I said..."

"I heard what you said. Please go to my mother's room and let her know I'm on the phone"

"ma'am, I "

"Never mind."

I pull into the parking lot at Sunshine and as usual, there are 58 empty spaces in the front, all marked 'handicapped.'

I slam on my breaks, back up, and head to the "visitors'" parking garage. Lord knows I am a believer in handicapped parking. I have to use it every month to take Jarvis to his appointments, but damn, you would think at a nursing home, someone would have thought about leaving a few spots for family that has to run in and out daily.

I am so tired and pissed that I have to park damn near a block away. I try to shake my poor attitude off and it is probably a good thing I have to walk this far before getting to my mother's room.

When I arrive at my mother's room, she is sound asleep. She looks very peaceful. I tiptoe to the head of her bed and smooth her hair, bending over I give her a light kiss on her forehead so I don't wake her up.

"*jMarie.*"

"Oh, Hey mom, I didn't want to wake you."

"I tried to call but they said you weren't taking calls. Are you okay?"

"Oh, yes, I was just tired and wanted to rest up today before going home tomorrow."

"Going home? Did the doctor say you can go home tomorrow?"

"I'm so sleepy *jMarie.* I'll see you tomorrow, okay?"

"Okay, mom. Jarvis wanted me to tell you hi and he tried to call you today too."

"Tell grandson I'll talk to him tomorrow, okay?"

"Okay, mom, I'll tell him."

"Goodnight, I love you."

"I love you too"

~~~~

In the bottom of the hall closet, I pull out four photo boxes. I wipe off the inch or so of dust that gathered over the past years.

Damn, I should have labeled these boxes with something else besides photos. Going through the first box, and oh, lucky, lucky me. I want to stand up and do the hallelujah dance, but I'm too tired.

I start singing "Hallelujah goes right there! Oh yes, my lord he works things out." Right on top looking and smiling at me is the photo of my mother and me just before my wedding. Jarvis is right; we look so pretty and we are smiling our little hearts out.

Turning the picture over, I run it back and forth on my nightgown to clean the dust off. I turn it over and then kiss it up to the sky.

Thank you, thank you, thank you Jesus.

I get in the bed, kiss my mother in the picture and carefully lay the photo on the pillow beside me.

What seems like only seconds later, I'm awakened by the phone. It says 2:22 a.m. My stomach ties itself in knots before I even answer it.

"Hello"

"Um, yes, um, is this *jMarie?*"

"Yes. Who is this?"

"Ma'am, this is the Sunshine Nursing home. I'm calling about your mother."

I squeeze the phone. I knew this was another one of those calls I never wanted to receive. Looking up to the ceiling I'm thinking, Lord, No! Please no. Lord, my mother loves you, is this how you're going to work it out? Is this how you are going to take away her pain? Lord, is this why she said she was going home tomorrow?

"Oh Lord, I wish I had known, I would have spent the night with her."

The voice on the other end said, "Ma'am are you there?"

"Ah, yes…um…was?"

"I was with her; she asked that I tell you she loved you." Then, she closed her eyes and peacefully went to sleep."

"Did you call my father and sister?"

"Ma'am your father is here, he came when you left last night. He was holding her hand as she was leaving."

"Is he okay?"

"Nurse Lydia is with him now."

"Lydia is with him?"

"Can I speak with her?"

"Well she is …"

"Never mind let her stay with my dad.

Thank you. Tell my father I'll be there shortly."

I hang up the phone and pick up the picture I had placed on the pillow last night. It dawned on me that the Lord did let me spend the night with my mother. He let me find the photo and it stayed on the pillow right where I placed it.

Jarvis is going to be so upset when I give him the sad news.

~~~~

Mother had made all the funeral arrangements, she always told us to bring her flowers while she was living and to bury her the same week she left for heaven. So here we are only three days later having mother's homecoming celebration.

Jarvis had a friend, who worked for the AAA plus van service, he was at the nursing home early in the morning to pick Jarvis up for his Grandmother's funeral.

"Man can you hurry-up I don't want to miss my Grandmother's service."

"Jarvis, your electronic bed is stuck. Let me call for another one."

"What do you mean stuck?"

"It won't go down so I can slide it in the van."

"Man, no… this shit cannot be happening today."

"Lord, I'm sorry, I don't mean to be cussing today, but please Lord don't let this happen today of all days."

Suddenly the bed begins making loud clicking sounds.

The aide's head jerked up as his eyes widened "There it goes, hey man, your prayer worked."

Jarvis smiles and says, "Thank you Lord, forgive me for the curse words."

"Ok man you're buckled in; did they put your meds in?"

"Oh wait, did you get the poem on my nightstand; I'm reading that at my Grandmother's funeral."

"Man, we're running late."

"I don't care, my mom wrote that for my grandma and my grandma loved it; I'm reading it today."

~~~~

The AAA Plus van service pulled up about five minutes prior to the time to march into the service.

Jarvis' mom and sister were seated in the front of the church. The aide wheeled Jarvis to the front so that he could see his grandmother. Jarvis asked the aide if he would kiss his grandmother for him. The aide was so kind; he bent over and kissed her. When he stood up, a tear was in his eye; he touched it with his finger and lightly placed it on the tear running down Jarvis' cheek. Jarvis said, "Thanks man, you're a real friend; now please push me next to my mom."

jMarie reached over and held Jarvis' hand until it was time for him to read the poem. Even though Jarvis could no longer be put in a sitting position, the aide and Nikita push his bed to the front alongside his grandmother's casket.

"Hey man will you hold the microphone and my sister can hold the poem up for me to read."

Jarvis clears his throat and begins reading. "This is my grandmothers' favorite poem. My mom wrote it for her but I'm changing the title for today from, A Mother's Love to "A Grandmother's Love."

"If I can't finish my sister will help me out; right Nikita?"

"Sure Jarvis, I'll help you. Do you want me to start it?"

"No, I said if I couldn't finish it."

"Well go ahead start reading." Nikita said as she lowered the paper for him to see.

A Grandmothers' LOVE is worth more than we can count.

A Grandmothers' LOVE never runs out;

Like an egg timer, whenever we need it

we just pick it up and set it down;

and the love starts piling up.

There may have been times in our lives when we may have argued with mother and our own egos,

Our own pride, would not allow us to humble ourselves and apologize;

and like an egg timer, we would set her aside until we needed her love.

But no matter how long we leave it on the shelf,

Grandmothers' LOVE is always there, never going anywhere;

so you pick it up, whether upside down or right-side up,

Grandmothers' LOVE starts piling up.

She has not lost an ounce of love,

And she is always there to start loving

over and over,

again and again

So no matter what we've said or done, we all know

A Grandmothers' LOVE is oh so dear,

A Grandmothers' LOVE IS ALWAYS THERE

The applause went on and on, I'm not sure if it was for the poem or the bravery it took for Jarvis to have his hospital bed wheeled to the front of the church and lay there and read the poem.

After the applause Jarvis glanced over at his mother and said "Forgive me mother, but I told you if you didn't copyright it, someone would steal it. Through his tears he smiled and winked at his mother.

As Nikita helped the aide move Jarvis bed back to his mother's side there was not a dry eye in the church.

~~~~

All for $898

A month after mother passed Jarvis asked if I would buy him an electric wheelchair. It was the first time he has asked for anything besides catfish and crab legs. I called a medical equipment sales rep the same day and they came to the nursing home with not just a catalog but they also had the newest wheelchair to hit the market.

Two days later Jarvis' chair was mistakenly delivered to my place instead of the nursing home. I couldn't sleep at all that night because every time I looked at the wheel chair I would start crying. And to make matters even worst, I got in the chair and tried to wheel it around the house, I kept bumping into everything. The more I bumped into things the more I cried. It was just the thought that the wheel chair was going to be my son's life. . . It was too much to bear. And I kept asking the forbidden question.

"Why? Why my son? I begin to wonder if this was how the Virgin Mary felt when she watched them nail her baby to the cross." I remember thinking she had to ask the Lord why her son.

Next thing I knew I had fallen asleep in the wheelchair and woke up early the next morning with my neck killing me. I took a long hot shower to relieve my neck pain and then decided to go shopping and surprise Jarvis with some new accessories for the wheelchair. I was just about to pull out of the garage and my phone rings.

"Hello."

"Yes, is this *jMarie?*"

"Yes, who's calling?"

"I'm calling about Jarvis, he was rushed to…"

"What do you mean rushed, rushed where?"

"Ma'am he was rushed to the hospital."

"Was? Why are you just calling?"

"Ma'am we left you a message earlier."

"I did not get any messages…never mind, what is wrong with him? Which hospital?"

"He was taken to Grant Road Medical."

"Ok, ok. I'll be right there. Tell him I'm on the way. Thank you."

I closed my eyes and said a quick prayer but suddenly I got the same nervous feeling I had last night when I was sitting in the wheelchair asking God why.

I begin crying and pounding on the steering wheel with the palms my hands. I pick up the garage door opener and let the garage door back down. I begin yelling at the top of my lungs. I felt like I was going crazy.

"Where are you Lord and where *were* you? Were you on daylight savings time when Jarvis was shot? Tell me where in the *hell* were you? You said you would be there in times of trouble; *that day was TROUBLE,* it was trouble with a capital "T".

Next thing I know I'm pounding my forehead on the steering wheel, the car horn goes off and I damn near jump out of my skin.

The sound of the horn quickly brought me back to my senses and made me calm down. I breathed deeply and let it out slowly. I breathed deeply again and held it, then let it out loud and slow.

With my head on the steering wheel I sat their thinking how it was just this week Jarvis showed any hope of getting out of the nursing home. He was grinning from ear to ear when he told the salesman he didn't want the model wheelchair he brought with him because he wanted the Cadillac version wheelchair.

I can see Jarvis face as he looked up at me smiling and said "Right mom, the Cadillac model for me."

Seeing him smile and that ray of hope in Jarvis is why I'm in this car headed to get accessories for his Cadillac wheelchair-- Now this call; he was rushed to the hospital.

I let the garage door back up, turn the rearview mirror so I can fix my makeup that has streaked everywhere. As I back out the garage a little too fast, I'm thinking-- It just doesn't seem fair--, nothing seems fair to me anymore…nothing.

~~~~

When *jMarie* arrived at the hospital Jarvis was still in the emergency room waiting to be seen. Soon as he sees me he starts yelling.

"Mom please get me the hell out of here. These pricks don't know what they're doing."

"Jarvis calm down, what is the problem; why did they rush you here?"

"Mom like I said these pricks and the pricks at the nursing home are so damn stupid."

"Jarvis, really you have to calm down."

"Calm down mom…; hell no! they don't understand calm."

"Well Jarvis they have the upper hand; you are at their mercy, try to be nice or at least civil."

"You're always nice mom, how the hell is that working for you…huh? Truth is I would be better off if they would just let me die."

"Jarvis"

"I'm sorry mom, I didn't mean it. I'm just tired of all the bullshit mom, really I am."

"I understand your frustration son. We need to talk about you moving home with me. I'm not good at the nursing stuff but I can learn."

Jarvis turns his head and smiles. "You know mom, that's the best thing I heard all day. You may be right it may be time for me to come home.   But you will need some help mom; remember you couldn't take care of my ear when I got it pierced and it swelled up."

"I know son, nursing wasn't one of my gifts. We can work all the kinks out and of course Nikita will help us."

"I love you mom."

"I love you too Jarvis."

~~~~

Turns out the reason Jarvis was rushed to the hospital is the nursing home had forgotten to remove the catheter clamp which caused him to suffer an autonomic dysreflexia, or something like that. The episode caused his blood pressure to go off the charts.

Jarvis said he didn't want to die in the nursing home, so he was ready to have the conversation about him moving in with me. He said a CNA who works at the nursing home has been visiting him late at night and said if I found a house, she would move in and do his nursing care for me.

Needless to say, after about five very hellish months of the CNA living with us, things just were not working out. Jarvis' Social Security checks came up missing and the house was never peaceful, it was always dirty. Half the time when I would call home asking to speak with Jarvis she would not put him on the phone and if she did let him speak with me, she decided what he could and could not say, she would hang the phone up in the middle of our conversations. She was 'evil' and I'm certain she was the devil's daughter. She was always mean to me and when she thought I wasn't around, I would catch her mistreating Jarvis. I told him it was time to get rid of her.

One day I came home and she was in Jarvis room with the speaker phone on. She didn't hear me come in so I stood in the hall and listen for a while. She had the Social Security Office on the phone and had Jarvis telling them he was agreeing to marry her and they wanted to know how much more the check would increase.

I pulled the telephone cord from the wall and told her to get the hell out.

Jarvis said "Mom what are you doing?"

"I heard your conversation when I was coming down the hall. I set your Social Security up and do not know why she is calling them. Your checks are directly deposited into your account. What is the problem?"

"Mom there you go minding my business."

"And just what does that mean Jarvis."

"Nothing mom and I am done with this conversation."

"No Jarvis we are not done with this conversation. I said why was she asking about your check?"

"You really want to know mom, huh?"

"Yeah, I really do want to know."

"For your information she has asked me to marry her."

"What! – I always knew she was up to no good, but this takes the cake."

"That's what you want? *jMarie* ask Jarvis almost in tears. "Mom, she said if we get married my check would increase from $898 to $1796 and she would give half the money to my son." "No Jarvis what she would do is take the money and run the hell back across the border with it, that's what she would do… you can bet her last tortilla on that shit."

I must have explained to Jarvis until I was black and blue in the face that she was up to no good. Finally, he agreed and we decided as soon as he was healthy enough we would move back to Texas. My friend had her own Unique Care nursing facility and she said Jarvis could stay for half the fee she normally charges. With all the stress we've been under, losing mom, the CNA moving in and causing way to much friction in the house, and several of Jarvis' Social Security checks came up missing. I think Jarvis and I were ready for a change. The challenge of course was over the next few months to get Jarvis healthy enough to travel.

Slow Traffic...Keep Right

Heading to the Lone Star State...

Jarvis' favorite nurse had a daughter who worked at the Village Inn located at the I-10 exit. She prepared a breakfast order for us to pick up on our way out of the city. We told our family and friends to meet us there for our last goodbye before heading to the Lone Star State.

After about 20 minutes of small talk, I noticed that the excitement we had just minutes ago was dwindling fast. Nikita suggested we hit the road to avoid another down pour of tears, and we all agreed. Thank goodness we did, because we were not two minutes on the interstate and I begin to cry. I look over at Nikita wiping away tears and trying to hide it by burying her head into her daughters. A quick glance in the rearview mirror and Jarvis has tears streaming down his face. His eyes are closed but you can see by the twisted frown and his facial muscles, he is saying "Don't say anything, just let me cry."

We were each, in our own way, experiencing hurt, and loss of what we were leaving behind; family friends and memories.

Jarvis tears reminded me about the time I took him and Nikita to the movies when they were younger to see E-T and how Jarvis was crying but didn't want anyone to know. That was the moment that I knew my son had a soft heart. As years passed and later when folks tried to tell me that he was a gangster, I knew that if he was, it wasn't on his own free will. I didn't say "No, not my son", but I did say "I'm going to find the person who has threatened him to be that way" As they say 2.5 million dollars later, the rest is history.

We drove in silence for what seemed like hours; then it was broken when Jarvis opened his eyes.

"Mom, are you sure we're going the right way?"

"Yes, of course I'm sure."

"Oh yeah, right mom!"

"No, really, one of the stipulations of the lawsuit was that the state would put signs up for me all the way from Arizona to Texas so as we pulled out of town with their 2.5 million dollars they could rest assured that we would never be back. I told them how important it was that we reached our destination as quickly and painlessly as possible for you Jarvis.

"They agreed to put up signs for me."

"How do you figure that mom?"

"See? Bending my head down slightly to look from under the rear view mirror, I point to my right. Smiling, I say "We've been passing them all the way. You didn't see them? "We just passed another one, you must of missed it. Wait, there you go, see that sign over there?"

"Only sign I see is, slower traffic keep right"

"That's it; you're right!"

"What? Slow traffic keep right."

Then Jarvis and Nikita suddenly got the joke,

"Yep. Slow sure would be your sign cause Mom, with your 55 mile an hour driving ass; I mean butt."

They all laughed.

"Don't you remember the old slogan '55 to stay alive'?"

"No Mom, we don't remember that. Let's see, was that horse and buggy days?"

"Ha, ha."

Nikita replied, "That was when she was teaching us how to drive. Together they both said, "Five miles slower than the speed limit or your ass won't be learning how to drive today."

"I know back then I did not use that word, I probably said your butt wouldn't…"

It felt so good as we all burst out in laughter again.

Knowing they were right, but not wanting to admit that I must have sounded so strict, I said, "Huh, I don't think I said that."

"Okay Right, Mom."

"Anyhow, as long as I follow the slower traffic stay right signs. I know I'll be going slow enough to not miss our exit."

"Hey ma, grandpop did a good job picking out the Winnebago huh?"

"Yep, he sure did. It's fully equipped, and over equipped with everything we needed. Even the air/float mattress for Jarvis had arrived just the day before we were ready to hit the road."

"Speaking of everything in it, Nikita will you put a movie in the DVD player?"

"What do you want to see? Everyone you know must have given you a video to watch for the trip."

"True Nikita and some of them are not for ya'll. So just look in the blue case and

get something my niece can watch too."

"Zoie has her Beauty and the Beast video in her teddy bear backpack, let's put that on."

Jarvis looks over at Zoie who has just woke up from her second catnap. "Hey pretty niece do you want to watch Beauty and the Beast?"

"Yes Uncle Jarvis, please."

The post-it on the dashboard slipped onto the floor, and thank goodness it fell, I forgot we needed to stop to pick up toilet paper; it was the only thing we forgot to get.

Spotting a Walgreens just ahead, I pull in and try to park this big ass Winnebago. At this very moment, I want to kick myself for letting Nikita and Jarvis talk me into driving instead of hiring someone to drive for me. After all, thanks to the Nursing home, I could afford a driver.

They convinced me that since Jarvis was feeling pretty strong and we were not in a hurry, I would be able to help Nikita drive.

"Mom, why are we stopping here?"

"Oh I forgot to get some tp."

"Mom we are grown-ass adults. You can now say toilet paper."

"Hey, your niece is with us, please watch your mouth on this trip."

"Oops, sorry. I forgot Zoie was in the car that quick."

"Ma, I'll go in and get it."

"Thanks, and Nikita, bring back my change."

Wondering what is taking Nikita so long, I look in the mirror and Nikita is standing in the parking lot smoking a cigarette. I blow the horn. She holds up one finger as if to say one more puff.

"Now I know why you were so quick to say you'll go in the store; I hope you didn't use my money for those cigarettes."

"I did, but I'll pay you when we get to Texas."

"Yeah, whatever Nikita just give me my change."

"Oh, there isn't any I got some candy and soda for Zoie."

"Nikita why would you buy the baby soda? Never mind don't answer; just sit down."

After driving several hours and the movie had been off I decided to turn on the radio, it was as if God were the DJ and he was playing our song "We've come this far by faith."

It was a long drive, but as we neared the next 5 exits to Georgetown, the sight of the ground covered with blue bonnets welcomed and excited us all.

Zoie yells, "Look at the rainbows Grammy!" As we looked up sure enough there was the most beautiful double rainbow, which was just another sign for us that said "we've come this far by faith."

First, we started off very slow and low as if we were singing to ourselves, then suddenly Nikita at the top of her lungs goes into the verse. "Just the other day, I hear a man say that he didn't, he didn't .. .and she drags it on, "believe in God's word, but I can say-- and all together at the tops of our lungs we all sing -- "That the Lord is the way, cause he's never, never failed 'us' yet." By the look on her brothers' face I could see he and I were thinking the same thing, that his sister is about to tear this song up just like she did when she was seven years old in Pennsylvania. We look at each other, smile and then Jarvis says "Ok, we're here. I'm going to take a nap now."

"In about twenty more minutes we will be at the house. Once we get you in the house and settled down, I promise I'll let you take a nice long nap."

"Ok, I'll hold off. I'll be pissed if I fall asleep, and then someone wakes me in twenty minutes. You're right mom, I may as well wait."

"Jarvis you know Moms driving, twenty minutes might be an hour an twenty minutes." Says Nikita as she reaches in her purse for a cigarette.

"Jarvis, Nikita, didn't the two of you see the sign we just passed?"

"Mom, it said twenty miles?"

"Oh… ok, but it won't be much longer."

"I hope not, because I need a cigarette."

"You know the rule still applies, no smoking in the house."

"I know, I know."

"Ok, just reminding you. We can stop in about twenty minutes."

~~~~~

As we turn into the driveway, suddenly Nikita says "I remember this street. This is where that lady with the big mansion lives, right up that little road over there, huh"

"Yep. Well she used to live there. She doesn't anymore; her daughter had to put her in a nursing home."

"Can we ride pass the house? I just want to look at it. It is so pretty. As we drove, it resembled a scene from the Extreme Makeover show. There were hundreds of people standing in the yard, holding up signs 'Welcome home Nikita and Jarvis'. Smiling, Nikita looks at her mom "Home? Is this the house you bought mom?"

"Yep! I knew we would all be happy here. There is plenty of room so that if we need our own space, we can each have that and my grandkids will have a huge playroom in the basement. Jarvis, you have your very own Physical Therapy room with a pool for some aqua therapy."

Unlocking the straps that are keeping the hospital bed from moving around, Nikita then pushes Jarvis hospital bed closer to the other window so he could see everyone outside the new home.

"Damn ! Are you serious mom?"

"Niiiiice !" Jarvis says as he drags out the –i-.

"I love you mom. I love you Nikita. Little Zoie come give your uncle Jarvis a kiss."

"Ok, I love you Uncle Jarvis"

"Uncle Jarvis loves you too and I'm happy we are all here together."

"Hey Mom remember when we were little and you always made me and Nikita hug and say I love you?"

"Yep"

"Well why did you always do that? Because half the time we didn't really mean it."

"That's right, because you were always mean to me Jarvis"

"No Nikita, you were always mean to me."

"Whatever."

"Hey, hey stop it. You see all those people out there waiting to cheer you up and welcome us to our new home. Get back in your happy moods."

Besides, it was okay at the time you thought you didn't mean it. Ya see, I knew that if something were to ever happen to one of us after an argument, the last words we would have spoken and heard were, "I love you." I never wanted us to go to bed and wake up to find that one of us was no longer here.

Then we would be trying to say that we didn't really mean those last hurtful words we may have said. Our conscience would rest assure that the last thing we said to each other was, as I turned to look at Nikita and Jarvis, "I love you."

You Can't Fix It

"You can't make everything right mom."

Moving back to Texas had several pluses for me. One was that Jarvis gets a new start, two, Senator Jane had won her bid for re-election and asked me to consider working for her again. Being with Jarvis had its good and bad days and some days I know Jarvis preferred we had some space between us. The other plus is my granddaughter Zoie is old enough to start preschool which means that Nikita will be able to help me out with Jarvis.

Lydia had called the other day to say she had just accepted a position as head nurse at Austin General and she planned to move out to Texas soon.

It is good to know that I will have Lydia close when I need a good laugh and besides she's one of the few nurses that Jarvis will listen too.

Lydia is an RN but I fondly refer to her as an AHC (**A**- **H**ypo-**C**hondriac) . Truth is she's a damn good nurse because she checks and rechecks *everything.* Sometimes she would tell Jarvis exactly which questions to ask the Doctor. I will never forget the time she actually gave Jarvis the wrong name for a condition. When he asked the doctor if he had it, the doctor laughed so hard, he actually thought Jarvis was pulling his leg. It turns out the condition Lydia told him to ask about was only something females would have. I'm telling you, only my friend Lydia the AHC, I mean the RN; could get that mixed up.

~~~~

"Good Morning, Senator Jane's office, how may I direct your call?"

Hello *jMarie*, Senator Jane here"

"Oh, hello Senator. How are you?"

"I'm fine, thank you."

"Is the office busy today?"

"Actually, it really is, since the morning news is all about your stand on President Obama's Health Care."

"Well please let my constituents know, I strongly stand for the health care package, just as the President has presented it."

"Oh yes, we also have been directing your constituents to your website to select the "We agree with Senator Jane" link.

"Oh, you added a new link to the web?"

"Yes ma'am. Thought it was a good way to track how many of your constituents were following the health care issue. I also added a mini poll regarding the transportation issue.

"That's a great ideal *jMarie*. What would I do without you?"

"Let's see. You would find about 10 college interns. No, just kidding."

"No, *jMarie* that is probably exactly what I would do. I'm so glad you are back."

"I am happy to be back Senator; I miss being able to run and see Jarvis whenever I want to but I'm sure he is happy for the break from me."

"Oh *jMarie* , I told you never worry about when you want to leave and be with him. Whenever you need to visit him or take him to an appointment or anything just do it. And I sincerely mean that; do you hear me?"

"Thank you Senator, I truly appreciate your understanding."

"I appreciate you updating my website. I almost forgot I was calling to ask if you would please email my flight information so I can forward it to my husband."

"No problem. I'll do that as soon as we hang up."

"Thank you and I'll talk to you later. Bye."

~~~~

It has been nearly two months since I returned to work and things at home have been going pretty good with Nikita looking after Jarvis. However, I had just walked out of a meeting when I received the call from Nikita that Jarvis is being rushed to the hospital.

I grab my things and head straight to the hospital. This is the second time since being in Texas that he has had to be rushed to the hospital.

When I arrive, Nikita and Jarvis are arguing about something.

"Mom, tell Nikita to go wait outside, I don't want her in here."

"Why, what's the problem?"

"The problem is your son is hard headed and don't wanna listen to anyone, that's the problem."

"They want him to get some physical therapy and suggest we put him in a state run nursing facility." Said Nikita

"Mom I don't want to go to no more State facilities." Jarvis said. "They don't do shit."

My first reaction is to agree with Jarvis. In the past they have caused us more heartache then anything."

I was just about to give my opinion when in walks a very attractive doctor who introduces herself as Dr. Lynn. She is very nice and convinces us to let Jarvis go to the State run nursing facility for the therapy that she says is much needed. I'm sure it is her good looks, more than anything, which has Jarvis all of a sudden changing his tune and now he wants to go to the state facility.

Nikita with one hand on her hip and her head doing the bobble from side to side says.

"Oh so now Blondie walks in and all of a sudden it's a yes. I just told you Ms. Lydia said, for a state facility it runs an excellent aqua therapy program, but you still said no. Now all of a sudden it's good enough for you."

"Nikita, I thought I asked you to go outside." Jarvis said to his sister.

"You did… I didn't… I didn't want to."

"Jarvis, Nikita stop bickering and let the nurse talk. I want to hear more about the aqua therapy program and how it will help."

"Mom, it's just a big pool, they put me in and it's supposed to help me walk."

"Walk!"

"Don't get excited mom, walking for me just means they put me in the pool and the water makes my legs flap around."

"Is that true Doctor?"

'Well if I may interrupt" She says. "Aqua therapy is good therapy to help quadriplegics from having their muscles stiffen and lock up on them.

"So you are willing to try this water thing Jarvis?"

"Yes mom, let's try it. But I'm not taking any shit from these state workers."

Jarvis looks at Dr. Lynn "I'm sorry, I didn't mean you Dr. Lynn, I mean those other folks I usually have to deal with."

~~~~

After almost eight weeks in the State facility, Jarvis has yet to have any aqua therapy session because he has not been feeling well. I get a call from Jarvis asking me to stop by after work so we can talk. In his conversation I could tell that he was trying to sound happy, but in his voice I could sense some fear. I decided to leave early and go see what he wanted to talk about.

When I arrive Jarvis was laying there with no TV or music on, his eyes were covered with towels and of course it was dark in the room. I open the blinds.

"Mom, is that you?"

"Yes Jarvis, I took off early, how are you feeling?"

"Not good mom. Please take the towel off my face so I can see you."

"Sure son." I take the towel off and bend over to give Jarvis a kiss.

"So talk to me son."

"Pull the chair closer to the bed mom."

"Ok, I just didn't want to knock the bed son."

"Mom, today a team of doctors came in and they told me I have about 3 months to live."

With a quick jerk my hand went immediately up to my chest as if to catch my heart from falling out.

"Jarvis, why … why did they say that."

"Mom there is a growth in my thigh and its cancer."

"In your thigh, same leg that was hurting last month?'

"Yes, mom the same leg they said nothing was wrong with it."

I'm afraid if I get up from the seat right now that all the tears will begin to spill out of my eyes and flood Jarvis room.   I need to get up and hug Jarvis, but I can't move.

"Are you okay mom?

"Um.. no son I'm not, are you?"

I finally stand up and begin to rub Jarvis head. …. "Oh my God, I don't know what to say Jarvis."

"Don't say anything mom, it's one of those things you can't fix."

But Jarvis…"

"Mom, I said don't say anything,."

"Mom call Nikita so she can come and be with you when you talk to the team of doctors."

"Did you tell her?"

"No mom, I'm only telling you, because my birthday is coming and I want a big party, I want everyone there, even the President of the NAACP. Don't tell anyone until I'm gone. Ok mom, please."

I swallow hard. "Ok son. Ok."

"You ok mom?"

"No son, I'm not, I can't imagine what you're feeling right now. I want to fix this."

"Mom, how many times do I have to tell you, you can't fix everything!."

~~~~

I did not call Nikita; I felt I needed to deal with this myself. Jarvis was being so brave that I wanted to be brave also.

I am yelling at the top of my lungs to the team of doctors who have summoned me in to discuss my son's failing health and to explain what the team decided would be the most comfortable treatment for Jarvis sake.

"How the hell…do you know it will be eighty days?

You don't know when God will say it's his last day! We have been dealing with his quadriplegia for these past five years and now you tell me my son has the "c" word…well screw you.!"

I get up and walk out. The meeting with the team of doctors has me exhausted. I head down the hall to the hospital cafeteria. My stomach is again in so many knots; food is not what I want right now. But I just can't head back to Jarvis room at this moment. I sit down and have a cup of coffee but then a strange feeling comes over me. Something tells me I need to get back to Jarvis room.

There was no one in the room with Jarvis; and he was throwing up. I grab a towel and the small pan on the nightstand.

I ring the nurse's bell for help.

He is throwing up every two minutes and no matter how many times I say "Stop talking, just relax, get some sleep" Jarvis ignores me talks a little more, and then asks me to throw cold water on his face. Then he throws up; it is green and slimy looking. I used up all the towels and need a nurse to bring in clean ones so that it will not get all over Jarvis.

I walk to the door and look up and down the hall for a nurse or anyone really. There's no one in site and I yell out "Where the hell is the damn nurse; I need more towels."

"Mom, stop. I don't need no damn towels. "

"But it's running down your neck."

"I can't feel it; it doesn't matter."

"But I don't want you to."

"Mom I said stop it! You can't fix this, no matter how many towels they bring you."

"But I…"

"Stop trying to fuckin fix it because you can't this time! Mom, it's time you learn three things, and learn 'em fast."

"What's that supposed to mean"

"It means, one, you can't make everything right mom. You jMarie Todd ; can't fix everything."

"And what's two?"

"Two, everybody don't want it fixed."

"And three…"

"Three everybody doesn't deserve to have it fixed."

"Okay, okay, I hear you, I got it. I'm just trying to make you comfortable; it's running down your neck."

"I told you I can't feel it."

"Ok, but I still don't want it to get all over you."

Scared and not wanting to cry in front of Jarvis, I yell.

"Son! You deserve to have this fixed."

"Mom, what I need fixed is to be able to walk through a park, to play football with my son, to reach up and hug and kiss my mom. That's what the hell I need fixed."

"I know son, I know."

"Well knowing it and being able to fix it; two different things!"

"Jarvis, son, I wish I could."

"Shut up mom! Listen, I love you mom; but stop trying because you can't fix this."

I am so hurt for Jarvis. I feel a flood of tears swelling up inside me. For Jarvis sake, I know I cannot let near a tear fall right now.

I say a quick silent prayer. "Lord please, please help me right now. Please hold this floodgate of tears back and let the right words come off my lips. Lord, I'm begging you please."

Jarvis is still yelling at me, and no one has come near his room. It has been close to four hours and not one damn person has bothered to come help me. Not one!

I am glad my dad has flown in to be with us. He was sound asleep in the very uncomfortable chair in the waiting room. I don't want to wake him.

Jarvis wants to sit up and I know it will be impossible for me to do alone.. Besides, he would yell if I barely brush against his arms so I knew if I tried to pull him up he would really scream… and I did not want to see him in any more pain; and I surely didn't want him to get any more upset with me than he already is.

I stop trying to wipe the vomit off his chest and decided to roll a towel up to place between his chin and chest.

"Mom, I'm sorry for yelling at you."

"Son, don't even mention it. I know you love me. I'm here for you; whether you want to yell at me, talk to me, laugh at me, sing to me or cry with me. It's all okay with me."

"Thanks mom. Will you please just rub my head real light like you were doing earlier?"

"Of course, like this?"

"Yes ma'am; that feels good mom."

"Do you want to get some sleep?"

"If I can stop throwing up I would like to get a little rest; then when I wake up maybe grandpa can help you sit me up. Then I can watch while you braid Nikita's hair today."

Jarvis has been throwing up for over six hours straight. When the nurse finally walks in, he asks her,

"How much time do I really have?"

"You may have thirty years, thirty months, and then thirty more years; only God knows dear. I can't answer that question."

She said it with such a sweet voice that I was glad he asked her and not me. Because if not her answer, at least the soft, smooth whisper of her German accent made Jarvis smile for a moment. I made a mental note to send a nice letter to her boss about her kindness. I quickly forgot she had left me alone with him for more than six hours straight.

A few hours later, I went to the nurses' station to talk with the doctor.

"Doctor he's been throwing up all night and all morning, what's going on?"

"Ma'am, over the next three days he will start to get worse.

Not wanting to hear anything else from the doctor, I turned and headed the half dozen or so steps back to Jarvis room. Jarvis was going on and on about how his sister's birthday was coming and we needed to throw her a party. He was mixing the birthday dates up between his, his son and his sister. I realize they were on his mind and confusing him, but it made him smile as he ordered me to not forget their birthdays and to have the parties.

Suddenly Jarvis had this far away look on his face. I screamed for a nurse to come help. When she arrived, she told me to take his hand because he was leaving. I don't even know if he heard me when I said "I love you." As a matter of fact, I don't even know if I said I love you out loud. I certainly know I was thinking it along with a hundred other thoughts.

The change in Jarvis was happening too fast. The nurse's words "He is leaving," hits me hard. I began rubbing his forehead and the top of his head the way he likes.

With my stomach feeling the exact way it was when I got that call five years ago that he had been shot. I was so ready to throw up. I can no longer stay in denial. My gut feeling said this is the time, and my heart was thinking, he's gonna see his grandma. Tears are filling my eyes and I say a quick prayer 'Lord don't let him see me cry, please don't.

I try to act like this is not happening, I try to talk, but caught in the middle of my throat are the words, "I Love you son and tell my mom I love her." My thoughts are interrupted when the nurse says

"Hold him; he can hear you, talk to him."

I cannot say another word because I realized he is heading home. I place my hand on his head and just keep slowly and lightly moving my thumb very gently across it.

Then the nurse says, "He's gone." I just stare at him peacefully lying there with his eyes open. I know he is gone but I still do not want him to see me cry.

A split second later, I cannot hold the tears back. I leave the room and run down the hall past the doctor who told me just three minutes ago that he would start getting sicker in three days. The doctor came running behind me, and followed me into the ladies room where I threw up my guts. He offered me some water and I offered him to get the hell out! And to go learn the difference between three days and three fuckin' minutes.

I Need to See You Say

...twinkle starlight twinkle

Today is the two month anniversary since Jarvis death. I woke up this morning craving some crab legs, and as I was standing in the fresh seafood section. (Which to tell you the truth, all looks like frozen seafood now thawed out). Jarvis' face was so vivid in my mind. I remember crab legs and powered doughnuts' was the last meal he asked me for.

It's as if it was yesterday and I remember the phone call about six months prior to losing Jarvis. I was in the car on my way home from work when he called me and said:

"Mom, I called to tell you what I want you to say at my funeral"

"Wha - what?"

Jarvis said "for my sons sake, I don't want a long drawn out service."

"Ok, what do you want?" I had asked him

"Do you have a pencil? I don't want you to get it wrong"

"Jarvis, I'll remember."

"Mom, just get a piece of paper and a pencil"

"Ok, I got it"

"First tell Grandpa thanks for all the visits, and I love him."

"Ok, is that all?"

"Yes, all the other stuff he knows. We had good talks."

"Ok. Next?"

"Tell my son I love him very, very much and to take care of his mother for me"

I remember trying so hard not to let him know I was crying and could barely see the car in front of me that day.

As I was trying to swallow the huge lump that was stuck in my throat. I wasn't sure if I could finish the conversation, but for his sake I knew I had to.

"Mom, did you get that?"

"Yep, got it. Go ahead"

"That's all. Oh, and tell my sister I love her."

"Ok. What do you want to say to me?"

"Mom, you know that I love you. Besides, everyone there will be saying nice things to comfort you."

"Ok. Son, you know it will be a rough day, but I promise you, when that day comes, I'll be strong for you and your son."

"Thanks Mom. I know I can count on you"

I remember asking Jarvis that day if we could talk about something else and he told me he was actually tired and wanted to take a nap. Before he hung up he asked if I would write him a poem like I did for my mom and read it for everyone and if I would bring him crab legs and powder donuts the next day. Of course I did.

I had never been so relieved to hang up a phone. That was the most painful call I have ever had. It was definitely one of those "did you know before you knew." Of course, if I did know that *that* was the conversation I was going to have that day, I would have never picked up the phone, but then, I would have missed getting Jarvis' final instructions.

Truly, sometimes it pays to 'not know, before you know.'

As I think back to the funeral, the Lord did walk me through it and I remember feeling like my mothers' angel was with me during the entire service as I read each of the statements Jarvis had given me six months ago on the phone.

I also remember the night Jarvis passed; I went through the rest of the photos in the four photo boxes I had pulled out the night he'd asked me to find the picture of his grandmother and me smiling at my wedding. I went through hundreds of photos all night, right into the morning hours. I cried, I laughed. I cried some more and laughed some more, I even ripped up a few of the photos I found in the boxes, (only because his dad was in the photos). I also laughed remembering the night he called his dad a 'sperm donor'. That was Jarvis, "saying the first thing that came to mind."

In the wee morning hours, and a few photo collages later, after putting all the photos away I set at the kitchen table and wrote this song for Jarvis. I was going to have Nikita sing it at the funeral but she had another one she picked out so I read it as the poem he asked me to write for his home coming celebration.

Why

Lord tell me why
Please tell me why
Tell me why you took
my only son.

I believed in you
even called on your name and;
prayer after prayer after prayer;

I'd hoped you'd be there.
But now I feel in my time of need;
you were nowhere near

Lord tell me why
Please tell me why
Tell me why you took
my only son.

Surely you knew
That a mother's worst pain. ..would run so deep
Losing my child...would not let me sleep
And tear after tear after tear
I wonder why
Why, you weren't there.
Where oh where
Oh where were you Lord?

Lord tell me why
Please tell me why
Tell me why you took
my only son.

~~~~

I recall following the celebration service for Jarvis, I was at my dad's house. There were too many people and way too much noise and laughter for me. I wanted to sneak out, go home, and cry until I had no more tears left. Turning the doorknob very slowly, I tiptoed out the door and let it close behind me. I heard a tiny voice.

"Grammy"

I turned around and my 4-year-old grandson had followed me out the door; he asked "Grammy, why did Jesus take your son?"

Not wanting him to see me crying; I pretended not to hear him and continue to walk to the elevator so he couldn't see me crying.

I remember thinking I wanted to say, "Why did he take your dad?"

I thought if I could shift the pain from me then I could comfort him for losing his dad. That would be so much easier. As I took two more steps to the elevator, the words of Jarvis hit me harder than a ton of bricks. "Mom you can't fix everything."

So I turned around tears streaming down my face and my grandson ran towards me and we hugged and we sat in the hallway and cried together.

That day, I had to face it; I could not fix my grandson's pain, I could not even fix my own pain. So together we sat on the floor in the hallway and let our tears flow for my son his daddy.

~~~~

"Hey *jMarie* looks like your daydreaming there, what cha going to have today?"

"You are so right I was daydreaming. The last time I was here, I was getting crab legs for my son."

"Yes I was sorry to hear about your son. Our lead butcher attended the services with our manager they said it was a wonderful service."

"Yes it was, and many thanks for all the crab legs you all sent for the service. Those who knew my son commented on how nice it was for your manager to send over so many crab legs that day."

"Well how many pounds will you have today?"

"Oh just enough for me. I'm going to eat a few in memory of Jarvis."

"Ok, do you want me to steam them with the lemon pepper he liked."

"You know, you are reading my mind; Thanks."

That evening after I enjoyed the crab legs I still couldn't get Jarvis or my mom off my mind. Feeling the need to be close to them, I pulled out my tablet and begin writing a poem that I could take to the gravesite.

I Need to See You Say

Have you ever placed a windmill at the grave of a loved one who's gone?

Did you ever say to the windmill? Turn windmill Turn

I need to see you say

You know I stopped this way today, you know I stopped this way.

Have you ever planted flowers at the grave of a loved one who's gone?

Did you ever say to the flowers; Sway flower sway

I need to see you say

You know I'm missing you today, you know I'm missing you.

Have you ever lit a candle on the birthday of a loved one who's gone?

Did you ever say to the candle; Flicker candle flicker

I need to see you say

You made a wish today, and your wish came true today

At the end of a lonely day, did you look to the sky and say, Twinkle starlight twinkle?

I need to see you say

You miss and love me too.

So Turn Windmill turn;

Sway Flower sway;

Flicker Candle flicker;

Twinkle starlight twinkle

I need to see you say

Happy Dreams

...dream dates with the "happy dreams."

It's Saturday morning and I just turned off the video from Jarvis funeral. I keep telling myself I will stop watching this every week, but every week it is as if I am addicted to the video. I feel as if I get my strength to move forward and it is a reminder that life moves on even when we think we can't move on.

Sometimes after watching the video I want to take a nap so that I can have what I like to call a 'dream date'. I just want to fall asleep and dream about Jarvis.

It seems dreams can have that funny way of making you wake up smiling, and you are happy all day long because the dream was just wonderful. I recall about a month ago, I had one of those dreams. It was nice because I went to sleep with a guilty feeling that I had not done enough for Jarvis when he was sick. In the dream Jarvis was lying on the floor in a pool of blood and we were somewhere where the ambulance could not get to him. So I pick him up, put him on my back piggyback style, and carry him out this window onto a very narrow ledge, tiptoeing very carefully across the ledge until I reach the ambulance. Just as we get to the ambulance, he whispers in my ear. "Mom, can we have a barbeque tomorrow?" I say sure. I will make some potato salad, and I know you want some baby back ribs. He looks up and says, "And some of those big beef ones and crab legs too; then he was quite for a moment, he cleared his throat and said mom I love you." Then he closes his eyes and dies.

Sad as it was, it turned out to be a somewhat happy dream for me. When I went to bed that night, I was thinking I wonder if Jarvis felt like I didn't do all I could for him.

Well you can imagine how I felt, not just the next day, but also all week long. Nothing and no one could upset me because I had this validation after my son's death, that I did do all I could and he loved me to the end even though I couldn't fix the worst thing that broke.

Unfortunately there are also times when you have bad dreams. I don't want to think about them…I like remembering my dream dates with the "happy dreams."

Chicken Wings

All I could think about was my auntie double dipping the chicken in some buttermilk ...

I want to say in all my years of living I don't think I ever learned so much so quickly as I did when I had first moved to this little old town in Texas. I like to refer to it as by-Georgetown because I found myself constantly saying, "By George, I didn't know this and by George I didn't know that.

Let me tell you, my girlfriends taught me that batteries were not just for radios, a little bit of dirt really won't kill you, and that pecans are just as good off the ground as they are in the bags in the store. In fact, I can say they are better straight off the ground.

I learned you really can leave the left-over fried chicken on the stove for more than an hour and still not get sick. Oh, and you can leave food in the fridge for more than three days and it won't kill ya either.

I learned that the things you buy from a garage sale can really be just as good as new if you just take them home and clean them up really good and no, you won't catch anything from them.

Now there's one thing, I don't do; I don't care what they say, I don't eat behind my kids, nor my grandchildren. I'm certainly not eating behind anyone else. I'm just that way. I got it from my mama. She said never eat or drink after anyone, nor use anyone else's comb.

Growing up as a child I remember that the neighbors moved out of the biggest house on the block, and they had thrown out toys galore. Aliza and I would go up this little alley and just look at the stuff. We didn't really want to bring it home; we were just amazed that someone was actually throwing these toys away. When my mother found us going through the toys, she made us go home, wash our hands, and take a bath. She said that we didn't know what those folks had. She said, "They may have roaches," and we might catch something. Mind you, my mother had the cleanest house I have ever seen. Folks were always saying "you can eat off your mom's bathroom floor, it's so clean." It was true and my mom sure deserved every one of those compliments.

I remember coming home from school some days to a newspaper trail leading from the front door through the living room the kitchen and all the way to the back door; where mama had just mopped and waxed the floors on her hands and knees.

Now for me, I prefer the motto I found on an old hanging plate I brought for five cents at a garage sale. The plate had been broken in three big pieces and glued back together. But the words on the plate 'Clean enough to be healthy, dirty enough to be happy." Quickly became my motto when I got older.

I remember every Saturday morning when we were doing our chores, I would keep reminding Aliza that when I got grown, I wasn't going to make my kids clean, and my house was going to stay dirty until I felt like cleaning it up. Of course, Aliza would agree with me.

We thought roaches was a disease for the longest time until once when we were visiting my cousins, and this bug crawled up the wall. My mom, said "Come on. Let's go.

Back then, and I am talking way back then, I was so skinny. Folks were always trying to feed me.   I was just fixing my mouth and my stomach to have some fried chicken and potato salad, because nobody could fry chicken like my auntie.

So I said, "But mom, can't we go after we eat?" She gave me that look as if to say; do you want to be spanked now or later? I remember Aliza yelling, "Oh, there it is again, that big fly must be hurt it's crawling"

Without even moving her lips, my mom said "That's not a fly- It's a roach."

Aliza and I looked at each other. Widening our eyes, then squinting, frowning and turning our nose up all at the same time, we both say "Roach." I whispered to Aliza, "I thought people got that when they were dirty and sick?" I don't remember what excuse my mom gave, but I do remember that we were out the door and headed home mighty fast.

I stayed mad because, that day, I never did get my chicken wings. All I could think about was my auntie dipping the chicken in some butter milk, then shaking it in the bag of flour which she seasoned with some *Lawry's*, paprika and salt & pepper. Then she would dip the chicken back in the bowl with the milk, and then a final dip in the seasoned flour. Just thinking about it, I can hear the grease popping.

Now that I look back, I guess I'll have to say that my auntie was giving her chicken an extra dip of hardening of the arteries.

~~~~

If this is Y-K-W

Christmas is my favorite time of the year and this will be the first time I won't be spending Christmas Eve with my family. I had a few hours to kill before heading down the road to pick up the Senator so I decided to go to the mall and pick up some last minute gifts. I wanted Nikita, Aliza and Lydia to be surprised when they got to the house on Christmas Eve to watch the "Hey Einstein" show. Seeing Vince there will be one surprise but seeing a gift on the table for each of them will help them get over the Vince surprise.

I'm going to be late picking up Senator Jane from the airport because there is an awful accident on the freeway. I always take the frontage road, but since I stayed longer at the mall than I anticipated and Senator Jane called and said that she needs me to pick her dog up before I get to the airport, I decide to take the freeway. I should have stuck with my usual routine and stayed on the frontage road.

Trying to tune the radio, I get nothing but static and more static. Ah, these country roads.

Wait, I think I got something. Oh, talk radio.

Damn, it's the racist guy. How ironic is it that his last name is 'Justus' which I think stands for "We like you if you look like us, you talk like us, you walk like us and of course, if you listen to us.

Granted, I turn his station on at least once a week for a very brief moment, but only long enough to be able to let others know that racism is alive and well. Sometimes we need to listen and hear what folks are plotting. I heard a politician say you need to know who is putting lipstick on their pigs and who is not.

Since we now have our first African American, black man, Negro, or to break it down for some folks, a "real" brother in the White House, it seems like racist folks are coming out of the woodwork like crazy. I have to admit, that we have more positive folks coming out of the woodwork then the negative ones. After all, President Obama would not have won if he were depending on the "black" vote. *I laugh to myself* because, yes, I think it, I say it and I know plenty other black folks know I'm right. They need to just admit it, and thank their white friends for voting for a "change" that we can all believe in.

Now I do not know what this nation will do when this younger, colorblind voting generation decides to resin the old rule, which states if one parent is white and the other is black then black it is.

I pray they will lobby for a law that says if you are of mixed blood, you can choose your race. Better yet, this colorblind generation (with a very large number of them mixed) may decide that there is only one race. Then we all have to check the little box that says "race" we will only have two options – Human Race- or Aliza's new word, Blood-lined ,which she said means your blood is lined with something else and who knows what. You gotta laugh just thinking about what folks reaction will be as they decide which box to check. Yes, I am with Aliza and the colorblind generation on this one.

Oh good, traffic is starting to move a little now, and there goes my phone. I am glad I programmed it to audio so I can hear the messages without having to pick the phone up and dial for the messages.

You have two new messages.

Bet I know the first one is "Don't forget to pick up the dog."

Message one from --Senator Jane

Hello *jMarie*, Jane here, I just wanted to remind you to please pick up my dog. Thank you, I'll see you at baggage claim.

Message two from--Senator Jane.

jMarie I know this is the week you go to California for the Hey Einstein Show. Wanted to check if you are still making sweet potato pies for us to enjoy while we watch the show. We invited friends to join us and you know my husband was bragging we were having your pies; besides it just isn't Christmas if we don't have your sweet potato pie. Let me know if you need me to pick up the yams for you. Oh, and of course, without *your* sweet potato pie it's not an official celebration of your winning; which we know you will..

I smile and make a mental note to myself...*type up sweet potato pie recipe and put in Christmas cards next year.*

The phone gives that last long beep... 'you have no more messages.'

Traffic is starting to pick up a little; I may only be a tad late. Of course, if the Senator is not at baggage claim, I'm sure I can find her at the nearest bar having a sip to relax herself.

I keep telling myself, I'm going to have to try the Senator's way of relaxation. It really does seem to work for her; she is one of the calmest people I know. Everyone's always telling me I need to "just relax." I might have to give her little trick a try someday soon, someday real soon.

Hmm, now seems like a good time to change my cell phone message while I'm sitting in this slow traffic doing nothing but tapping my fingers on this steering wheel. I put the car in park and grab my phone. I put the windows up so the outside noise won't interfere while I'm recording my message.

I'm thinking I should do my Christmas message to remind everyone that the gift of Christmas has already been given. And of course I can add my usual Happy Birthday Jesus.

On second thought… let me just do a quick one and maybe change it later.

Hey, you reached me. ..um..Oops.

Hit star twice to re- record message.

Hey, it's not you so it's gotta be me…

I start singing…*it's gotta be me.*

Okay, I tell myself to stop playing around and record the message.

I hit star twice to re-record.

Hey there, it's me, sorry I miss your call, but here is your thought for the day "Did you know, before you knew" Think about it… if you knew you was going to get my message machine, then you would not have called and you my friend-- would have missed out on the thought for the day, which is, treat yourself to something wonderful, I'm sure you deserve it.'

Nah, that's too long. Let me try one more time.

'Hey! Its jMarie, sorry I missed your call. "At the tone… convince me to call you back. If this is 'you know who' I'm already convinced."

The phone goes beep. ..Satisfied with your greeting press pound, to re-record your greeting hit star.

Ah, I like it, especially since I know Lydia and Aliza will hate the line "If this is you know who."

Laughing out loud, I press pound.

The phone voice command says 'callers will now hear your new message.'

Making Sweet Potato Pie

"This pie is something to sink your teeth into"

I'm glad Senator Jane reminded me about her pie. I had forgotten that I promised her I would make her a pie before I left for the show. Besides Aliza, Nikita and Lydia were looking forward to having their get together at my place and I promised I would have a pie waiting for them.

Being at the Hey Einstein finale, I will miss the church Christmas party and I've been promising the pastor's wife I would make her one of my famous sweet potato pies. I swear, for a white girl, she makes the best greens I've ever tasted. She promised to cook me a pot of greens if I make the pie so, I think this year, she just may have herself a deal.

It's time I make good on the aging , yellowing, and tearing newspaper article that hangs so proudly, by one thumbtack, in the church vestibule "This pie is something to sink your teeth into" the article carries a quote from the famous Emmy award winning actor Louis Gosset Jr. "Don't share her pie with anybody, it's like gold". Of course pastor's wife keeps reminding me that she has no intentions of sharing her pie, so I will need to make her one for herself. No problem, I get a pot of greens she gets a sweet potato pie, fair and square. Nah! I think I got the better deal, a whole pot of greens. Yeah, I win.

Its Friday rush hour traffic. I just want to get home, kick off these high heels and let the TV watch me fall asleep, but no, I have to stop and pick up about eight medium yams. I don't know why they don't call it a yam pie because yams are the best potatoes to use.

Well, well, well, what do you know? Staring me right in my face is "today's special" aisle 3, Keebler™ ready-made pie shells" 99cents…yes! Since I already had the stuff to make the pies to leave at the house, I needed to get ingredients for two more pies. I pick up two shortbread "Keebler™ pie crust." I'm glad they were on sale today, but let me tell you, just go ahead and spend the extra fifty-cents and get the name brand. I've tasted some pies with the other crust, well….let me just say this one more time. "Spend the extra fifty cents for the name brand." Speaking of using the name brand stuff, why is it that every time the white or brown sugar is on sale it's "not" cane sugar. Damn, I don't need 5lbs of sugar; I don't care if it is on sale, oh well… I just need the one pound boxes, since I only need a little of both.

I hate carrying those little shopping baskets so I grabbed this big shopping cart like I'm about to shop for a weeks' worth of groceries. Let me see, I need a half pound of "real butter" yes "real butter". I'm not even trying to skimp by using 'margarine.' Not for my pies. You will also need a small can of *carnation evaporated milk* (you only need about a quarter cup, if you desire more, just add a little at a time). Let's see, I'll need two eggs. I hope I can find a ½ dozen, last time I was in this store I decided to split a dozen cartoon in half, when I got to the counter the chick tells me they don't sell just a ½ dozen she'll need to get a price check. I said "hell they're seventy-nine cents a dozen. You can use the SCS (school of common sense) method, add a penny, that makes it eighty cents, now, divide that in half…but no, she couldn't do that, it was too damn simple. I'm not sure to this day which it was, she couldn't add and subtract or she just preferred to make a scene because I split the damn cartoon of eggs in half.

Spices, spices, spices, I can't remember if I have enough pure vanilla (not imitation) and I'm hoping there is at least a tablespoon worth of both vanilla and cinnamon at the house. Okay, that's everything, let me pick up about six yams and get out of here. I pop the tip off at least five of the yams and everyone is just dry inside. Just in case I have to use sweet potatoes, I pop the tips off two and they are dried up as well. This will not work, damn! I don't know why I keep kidding myself that this time I'll find good yams on this side of town. I have a notion to just leave this cart with all my stuff in it and head to the foothills, where it looks like some farmer may have just dropped off his freshly picked fruits and vegetables.

I hate making two stops, let me go ahead and pay for this since I have everything I need but the yams and the can of pecan icing.

~~~~

Back at the house I put on Patti Labelle's "If Everyday Could Be Like Christmas." I start singing along with Ms. LaBelle. I grab the potato brush and begin cleaning the yams. It didn't take long to clean these yams, which actually already looked pretty damn clean. My trip to the foothills was worth the gas.

Reaching under the cabinet for the large pot to boil the yams.

"Shit", no one but my lazy sister done put these big ass pots on top of the small pans because she's so trifling. I swear, I'm going to stop letting her come by when I'm not here. For someone who works out all the time she sure can be lazy around the house; I mean the girl is just plain lazy.

I fill the pot with enough water to cover the yams and let them cook until they get soft. I always cook the yams with the skin on because it adds so much more flavor and vitamins to the pie.

Searching the cabinet for my mother's big white mixing bowl, which isn't where I last left it. I swear it may not be worth it, always telling Aliza I'll cook, if she'll clean up. It takes me a month of Sundays to figure out where she put, or didn't put, my stuff.

Finding the bowl, I place two sticks of butter and a tablespoon each; of vanilla and cinnamon in the mixing bowl. When the yams are done, I'll peel them and drop them right on top so they'll melt the butter.

Ooops let me put out some "food handler" gloves so I can peel the yams. Now Lydia will tell you that you can use those gloves that they use in the hospital room, and they're cheaper by the boxes. I keep telling her that those gloves are not sanitary enough for me, and you know she just laughs, she may be right, but I still want the ones that were made to handle "food", not the ones made to assist in wiping someone's behind. Just doesn't sound right to me. Tell ya what, if I didn't have the food handlers' gloves, then I just go ahead and use me two sandwich baggies, I know they are made for food; so they work just fine for me. Okay, enough about the damn gloves, where is my grandmother's potato masher? I've been told that it's much easier to just use the automatic mixer, but I have it made up in my mind that my grandmothers potato masher is by far much better, and it will allow me to not overbeat my yams. Now for the sugar… hey, sorry, I have to talk (to myself) while I cook; that's why I don't like anyone in the kitchen with me. Folks hanging around will mess up my train of thought and the next thing I know I forgot what ingredients I did and did not put in my food. So where was I? oh yes, the sugar, now I always start with one cup of brown and a half cup of white sugar, you can then season, as my mother would say "to your taste" as you go. If the yams are not very sweet, I may add more vanilla instead of more sugar … helps keep the calorie intake low… laughing aloud. Beat your two or three eggs really well add them along with your quarter cup of evaporated milk. Pour into your two prepared Keebler™ pie shells and bake at 350 about 55 minutes. I judge my doneness when the pie looks like it is puffing in the center.

While the pie is cooking, I open a can of pecan icing and put in a medium bowl, add additional walnuts and or pecans and coat the nuts well. During the last five minutes of cooking time or you can wait until completely done, add the topping. Because the topping makes the pie extra sweet you do not want to cover the pie, just around the edges is good.

The winner is...

_____

I felt like I jumped 30 feet in the air. A quick shake of my head
helped me realize I was awakening from a dream. I looked around
my small bedroom and was relieved to see familiar surroundings. I
shot a quick glance at the alarm clock and it read 6:09am.

"Oh shit!" Staying up late to bake the pies last night had me
running late this morning.

Hopping around on one foot, I slip my leg into my shorts and
then slip the other leg into the same short leg. Losing my balance, I
fall back onto the bed. Yawning, I stretch my arms, fold my hands
and pillow them under my head, I close my eyes, and think, aah, this
feels good.

Looking out the window it looks like we will have a nice wintery
warm day. I'm a little upset that I already missed seeing the sunrise
display its mysterious shadows across the mountains.

Okay, okay, get your butt moving. It's Saturday morning and
you are already running a half hour late.

You need to get your walk on so when you pick up Ms. Fitness
addict Aliza, at the airport you can tell her, no you're not going to the
gym, you already walked. I am not mad at Aliza, she lost over one
hundred pounds in less than a year; she's still losing weight and she
looks great.

On second thought I really do think I'll skip today's walk. I have way too much to do. Besides, that kid has probably already let his two big ass dogs crap on the walkway, not even bothering to stop and clean up behind 'em.

Ah, speaking of shit, I need to pick up those –half the time, don't work for shit, cameras so I can get this last photo shoot done. I need to submit my hairstyles for the BET hair contest" It's Your Hair! or *Is it* Your Hair?" contest deadline is in just two days when I return from the 'Hey Einstein' show.

I feel it in my gut; I'm going to win that million dollar invention of the year award. I swear the first waste of money will be to hire me a chauffeur, cause Lord knows I hate driving. Hell, I'm busy thinking about my next new hair style and trying to think for the guy ahead and behind me who is not thinking. It just drives me nuts, no pun intended. Besides, I like to be the passenger so I can look at the sky, the trees, the water, and the birds, whatever.

Let me check my emails so I can get outta here.

Not enough connectivity notice pops up on the computer

What the? I have a mind to call and complain about the internet connection constantly going in and out. Hell, I don't see the bill coming and going; she laughs to herself, but it's not funny.

I need to find driving directions to this shoot or I know I will get lost. I turn the computer off and count to myself one; two, three and I turn it back on hoping this would do the trick. At least that is what I was told by my IT person.

Not enough connectivity, please try again later.

Shit. Maybe on my next check I'll write in the amount line

"Not enough money, please try again later"

jMarie abruptly ends this crazy thinking and heads to the shower with her prayerful song in her lungs…"I woke up this morning, as I walked to my shower…on my own… two… feet, I was singing; Hallelujah goes right there!

Hal..le..

'Ding…"You got mail."

Oh, figures. Now that I'm about to step in the shower it wants to connect.

I quickly step backwards to get out the shower, forgetting it's wet and I slip and stub my toe. "Shit! Damn it!" I tiptoe to the desk and the computer screen shows there are twelve available Wi-Fi's." Great let me try one of these… It asks for a password! Damn."

jMarie is glancing down the Wi-Fi list when she sees a really strong connection showing about 8 bars, but the name is NOinternet4U2day. "Ha ha ha that is some funny shit." Continuing down the available list, "linkIt " comes up but the message pops up again, password required. Nearing the point of giving up when she spots 'OkUMoochersOweMe1' clicks on it, and ta..da… she's in. Yanking my right arm up with a closed fist I pull it down quickly doing a Tiger Woods "YES!" and Google the location for my photo shoot.

Headed back to the shower, I'm singing even louder, happy I now have step by step, turn by turn, directions to where I'm going.

At the top of my lungs …

"My, my… my Lord…he works things out!"

~~~~

The photo shoot took four hours longer than I had anticipated, or did it? I knew the cameras were going to be a challenge, and I should have filtered in a couple extra hours for retakes. Oh well, let me stop complaining. It's done and that's the important part.

I must admit it felt good these past months getting back into the swing of exercising and working on my invention. I was even excited about getting the call from Vince and looking forward to going to California together.

After losing my mom and my son, life took its toll on me and I couldn't think for myself, much less think about my invention. I'm glad Aliza did submit my *ez*Hook*it*. Now I have jumped back in with both feet and some days I think I may have bit off way more than I can chew. That's okay though. I am determined that once again, this is the year for me to come into some good luck and winning inventor of the year is definitely at the top of my goal list.

I'm going to stop by my storage to pull out some more of my invention stuff and get new hair extensions to take to California for the show. I see the Patti collection now has a variety of color hair in human hair and I want to submit a couple hair styles using the human hair. Gotta do that for all the brothers who think the "long blonde hair" they see is "real".

I swear, no matter how many times a sista tells the brothers, "All that blonde or long hair probably came from various resources," the brother still don't believe us. They never believe us… oh well.

~~~~

jMarie was going to California a couple days prior to the Live finale show of "Hey Einstein." She told Aliza and Lydia she did not need a ride to the airport because she was taking the shuttle. Truth is that Vince had his year end fraternity meeting in LA , so they were going to fly to California together. He was then coming back to Texas and stay at her place.

~~~~

At the hotel I decided to take a shower and a quick nap. I'll call the ladies before I head to the show tonight, I do not want to hear all they have to say, once they get to the house and find out that Vince is there. They will be surprised, but they will get over it quickly once he pops out the champagne he brought for them; and they see the new TV he got me for Christmas.

I'm on cloud nine after my dinner with Vince, and I never in a million years was expecting to get engaged. I sit on the edge of the bed starring at my engagement ring. I felt like a teenager who just received their first friendship ring. Kissing my ring, I lie down and reminisce about when I first met Vince.

It was the annual Charity gala. Vince walked in the room and I spotted him immediately. He reminded me of a soft and cuddly teddy bear. I felt an irresistible attraction to him (and I don't mean sexually). When I finally decided to take the plunge and ask him to lunch. I felt comfortable, since I do not think about sex in the daytime. To be honest, it had been years since I even thought about sex.

I had asked him if he was seeing anyone.

His response was "You know I'm available."

Turned out available meant something entirely different to him, than it did to me." We had been dating about three months when

Lydia called to tell me that she had seen him in the club with someone. When I asked him about it; he replied with "Sweetheart, when I go out of town sometimes I date."

My reply to Vince was "Well, I guess as long as it's not here, in-town, I can deal with it; and if it gets to be too much for me, I will quietly walk away."

Because I certainly have very high self esteem, in my heart I believed he would stop going out of town and realize that I was all he needed. Silly, silly me.

It was funny, seeing an email with Vince's name on it would make me suck my stomach in and clench my thighs so tight, I would almost stop breathing; I swear he gave me a feeling that I never had before, when I told Lydia she said I was "horny" well at fifty-one, I must admit I don't think or remember ever being horny before. If this was the way Vince was making me feel, I definitely knew I was scheduling that doctor appointment I kept putting off.

"Besides", I told her, "I don't think that's what it is because I never even think about sex."

I told her I enjoy his company so much; I could spend the rest of my life with him just talking and holding his hand. She said "yeah, but sex can be the icing on the cake". I told her maybe so, but I was only interested in pound cake. She swore she was going to hang up the phone, but she did not; knowing she had some more gossip to share. Then she said I needed to get out more often and meet more folks.

I didn't tell her this, but my thought was I don't ever need to meet another person until it's time to meet God, because if Vince was the last person I ever met I guess I was fool enough to think my life was complete. He was the only person who ever called me 'sweetheart and darling'.

Lydia said he probably called everyone that so he did not get the names confused.

Sitting here thinking back, I admit, it still made me feel good when he called me sweetheart.

I'm glad I told Vince I realized I had asked too much of him when I negotiated with him that I would always be there for him if he protected my heart. I let him know that protecting my heart was my job."

It was one of the bigger lessons I learned after I released myself of a fifteen year relationship that I was committed to and the only thing I got out of it was a broken heart. My to-do list started looking like:

#1. Take care of your heart. #2. Take care of your heart.

#3. Take care of …well you get the picture, and thank goodness so did I.

I realized that getting mad enough forced me to do what was best for me, so I committed to be a better guardian of *my* heart.

While trying to work out whether or not to continue seeing Vince we agreed to be platonic friends until he was not afraid of the "c" word. He knew I meant "c" as in "commitment". It wasn't long after that conversation he left a message on my cell. It was the Luther Vandross song, *"I'd Rather"*

Then Vince's voice comes on "Hey Sweetheart, I hope you are listening to those words…"I'd rather have bad times with you, than good times with someone else." I woke up missing you, and I think I'm ready for that other "c" word, what about dinner tonight? Call me if you're available."

Looking at my engagement ring; I'm glad that I called him back six months ago.

I don't know how long it will take me at *-getting good-* at caring for my heart, because I've spent most of my life trying to take care of everyone else's heart. Trust me, my ass is looking forward to 52, because I know I'll spend every day challenging myself to guard my heart while taking care of it. Just saying it puts a smile on my face.

~~~~

After arriving at *jMarie*'s house and getting over the shock that Vince was there sleeping on the couch. Nikita, Lydia and Aliza have fried up some catfish and chicken wings and already cut into the sweet potato pie *jMarie* left for them to enjoy while they watched tonight's show.

They have finished sending text messages and photos of their hairdos to *jMarie*. They are now ready to settle in and watch the inventor of the year finale episode of the "Hey Einstein" show.

~~~~

Sitting here waiting to go on stage, I pull out my phone for one last look of the pictures the ladies sent me. My heart wishes they could be out in the audience but we just couldn't arrange it in time.

They have all used my "*ezHookit*" and styled their hair into upsweeps. They even added purple and gold highlights to celebrate the grand finale. I told them if I win I would start each of them out with their own "aNeatLook" franchise mobile hair salon.

Vince texted me with our I Love You code (45888). It made me smile. I'm so happy we're together again. Vince went out and brought me a 72 inch flat screen TV. I'm not sure if it was a Christmas gift, a back together gift; or a nice way to watch the football season for him. He also knew the ladies would be there to watch and record the Hey Einstein show for me. I think he may have wanted to earn some brownie points from them.

Rightfully so, my friends believed me when I told them this is my year, and I'm not taking second place in anything, not my job, not my man and most importantly I'm praying I won't be taking second place in the inventor of the year award.

~~~~

"Sh…sh..."

"Okay, it's on. Cross your fingers."

"Okay"

"Third place goes to James and Jim, the candy maker machine."

"Don't call her for second place man. Please don't call my mom for second place."

"Don't call my sweetheart for second place."

"Vince we'll need you to save the lovey-dovey stuff for *jMarie*."

"Come on ladies, that's what I would say if she were here."

"I'm sure you would, but she's not here… it's just us"

"Ok…shh."

"And now for our second place J… "

As if they were triplets, the ladies all at once, sucked in some air, held it and grabbed their chests.

"Jane Hall, the baby car-sleeper."

"Oh, my God, oh my God, I thought he was going to say *jMarie*."

"Ok, ok, this is it! It's either her or the guy with the talking toilet seat."

"Come on man, come on. Just tell us."

Now they are all on their feet locked in a straight line of hugs, ready to do the "Hallelujah dance."

"Vince, come on you can join us, we are about to do the 'hallelujah dance."

"She's one of the last two standing"

"Thanks, but I'll pass on the dance."

"Come on Vince."

"Yes, come on Mr. Vince it's for my mom."

"Ok."

"Shh, here's the announcer; hold on."

"Our final two contestants have both won previous awards for their inventions presented here tonight. On my left is Jon John, (no pun intended), it really is his name. Jon John received second place for the Bathroom Gadget of the Year award and *jMarie*…"

"Hey, did you notice all the finalist names begin with the letter "J," how strange is that?" said Nikita.

The announcer grabs *jMarie's* hand. "And on my right we have *jMarie* who took first place in the *BET* 'It's Your Hair or *Is it* Your Hair' contest. And the winner is…

"We'll be right back after this commercial break to present our million dollar check to our invention of the year recipient."

"Come on! Damn!"

"Another commercial?" says Nikita all frustrated.

"Ladies, come on. You know how TV drama works; you always get the answer after the commercial break." They have to pay the announcer who says, "We'll be right back with our winner, after this commercial break."

"Oh, thanks for reminding us Vince."

"Don't mention it; that's why I'm here."

"No, you are here because my sister has conveniently forgotten to tell us you were staying with her." Says Aliza

Lydia raising her glass for the fourth time "But that's okay Vince; she loves you, we love you. Now pour me another drink please."

"Thank you Lydia, now everyone get your glass because I told *jMarie* that we would be having a champagne toast to her winning."

"I got a toast for my mom."

"Even if you didn't, I bet you're going to drink huh?"

"Ha ha, very funny, but seriously, remember how my mom always says to count our blessings, because just when we feel we're going through hell on earth, along will come moments that will make the flames of hell dwindle and turn to ashes or something like that."

"This toast is to my mom and 'dwindled flames' or ashes or something."

Lydia looks at Nikita and lifts her glass, "to dwindled flames."

"Good one, and now let's toast our friend slash soon-to-be-business partner."

"Sounds good to me" says Aliza as she clicks her glass with

Lyida.

"I'll drink to that one too" Nikita says holding her glass up for Vince to pour her another drink.

"Dang Nikita, are you trying to keep up with Lydia?"

"Nope, guess I'm just missing my moms."

"Well let's toast to my soon to be wife."

"What?"

"Did you just say what I thought you said?"

"Ah, *jMarie* didn't tell you?"

"The waitress took a picture with her cell phone at the restaurant and *jMarie* said she was going to send it to your phones."

"Mr. Vince you know my mom does not know how to do that."

"Wow my sis is engaged?"

"For real? Wait…when?"

"I was with her in California last night, I asked her then."

"Well Lydia, my sister did tell us she wasn't taking second place to her man this year."

"That is what she said Aliza, and I'm not mad at her."

"Hold on, my mom's back on…hold that thought."

"Ok"

The ladies and Vince are holding their breath, standing in front of the TV with their arms interlocked and holding their drinks.

Nikita says "ok everybody cross your fingers."

Lydia looks at Nikita and says "Just how do we cross our fingers, we're holding our drinks."

"Try something new Ms. Lydia and cross your legs."

"Whoa! A little too much to drink there missy." Aliza says to her niece. "Ms Lydia is your elder."

"My bad… I was just playing Ms. Lydia; I'm sorry."

Spotting his phone on the coffee table, Vince breaks from the line to grab the phone.

"Ladies, hold that pose, *jMarie* is going to want this Kodak moment!"

"Say cheese."

There is no response from the ladies.

"Ok, say sexy."

"Ladies come on, could you look over here please."

"Shhh."

Trying to get the ladies to look his way Vince says "Wow, this is more than a Kodak moment, you are not even talking."

"Shhh."

" Really Vince hush and turn the TV up louder"

There's a dead silence.

"And the winner is. . .

jMarie, owner and hair artist of aNeatLook Incorporated."

Still hugged in a line, they all forgot about the drinks in their hands. Champagne flew everywhere as they were jumping, crying, laughing, kicking their feet and shouting.

Vince starts snapping pictures; everyone is laughing, posing and flipping their pony tails from one side of their shoulder to the other.

Vince said, "Ok, everyone raise your glasses so I can get the champagne toast picture I promised *jMarie;* and what's the song *jMarie* made up? – I worked it out or something."

"The one ya'll keep singing."

"Hallelujah goes right there?" says Aliza, and she repeats under her breath " because my God sure did worked this out."

"Oh yeah that's it, so excited Vince starts singing "My wife, she worked..."

In unison, the ladies turned their heads slightly, tilted their shoulders, bending their heads and glared at Vince. "Just take the picture Vince."

"Ok, than you ladies; *jMarie* thanks you also."

With her hands on her hips and shaking her head like she does so well; looking like a human bobble head, Nikita says "Hey Mr. Vince, I think you meant to sing , my mom worked it out, right?"Nikita sings the verse at the top of her lungs.

With a high kick in the air, Aliza throws two air punches, no "my… sis!" is what he meant to say.

Lydia picks up the champagne bottle "Ladies, ladies, give the brotha a break."

"Thanks Lydia" says Vince. "I was repeating the song and I meant to say …"

Before he could finish, as they are laughing and crying the tears of joy, all together they sing it out… ***"My Lord, he worked it out; Hallelujah goes right there!"***

###

About the Author

Being the third of twelve children, I'm ever so grateful to my parents who taught us that if God brought us to it, then with Him we would be able to go through it. They taught us also that by believing and keeping (at the very least) a mustard seed worth of faith we could come out of the fires, and folks would not even smell the smoke on us.

My parents had such loving and giving hearts, I thank them for passing those genes on to me. However, later in life, just short of turning fifty, I realized that an always loving and giving heart can sometimes be the thing that destroys it, both physically and mentally.

So to my readers, please know (in my opinion) that one of the hardest jobs in the world, is "Guarding Your Heart" and ONLY YOU will be the BEST person to fill that job with your highest level of satisfaction. It is, after all, your responsibility.

Single parents, It is also my opinion that you have the other hardest job.

~~~~

For my family and friends who are always asking me to bake them a pie, so you will not have to grab pen and paper when you are reading the Making Sweet Potato Pie chapter I've include my recipe which Grammy award winning actor Louis Gossett Jr, told a reporter at the *Tucson Citizen*, and I quote "Don't share her pie with anybody, it's like gold."

Anita's Sweet potato pie

1- 9' Keebler ™ shortbread or graham cracker pie crust
4-6 med yams or sweet potatoes-
Clean yams, cover with water and boil till soft. Peel and drop hot yams on top of ¼ to ½ cup Butter (not margarine) add 1T pure vanilla   1T cinnamon
Mash with potato masher then add
¼ c pure cane brown sugar and ¼ c pure cane white sugar (add more sugar or vanilla to your taste) *add*
2 eggs *(whisked)* and ¼ c evaporated milk *(may not need all the milk).*
 Mix thoroughly place in pie shell and bake at 350 *about 55 minutes. When done pull pie out and add pecan/walnut topping around edges of pie.*
 ~~~

Pecan/Walnut Topping
1 small bag shelled walnuts
1 can Pillsbury Pecan icing
 using ½ can of the icing add walnuts until they are well coated with the icing. Carefully line the edges of the pie with topping.
~~~~

Dear Reader,

I've added this book bonus "Responsibility" just for you. I had to learn or maybe re-learn that "I" am responsible for my happiness. Just as I had finished writing this book, I was cleaning out one of my "catch-all drawers" and I came across a little pamphlet I wrote about 15 years ago. Even though it took me ten years to finish "I Need To See You Say", I'm thinking I would not have finished had I not taken Responsibility one letter at a time.

I'm grateful and thankful that you have taken the time to read my book. If you have comments you like to share, please send me an email at 2CUSay@aneatlook.com

I Love to hear from you.

Anita

R-E-S-P-O-N-S-I-B-I-L-I-T-Y

Recognizing that **y-o-u** have a choice

Expectations can only be met when they're fulfilled; Promise what
you can deliver

Set your boundaries; only you know your schedule

Priorities; Include your own.

One day a week belongs to Me

No= Negotiate an Offer . . .It allows you to say "YES to Y-o-u

Satisfy yourself first; then others

I "I" am a responsible person

Believe you need YOU too

I "I" will take responsibility

Loving yourself has a domino effect; feel good about YOU; you feel
good doing for others

I without "I" "I" and "I" there is no responsibility

Tolerate the things YOU want ; not what others want you to.
We deserve what we tolerate

You must take time for Y-O-U;

Hang out your DO NOT DISTURB sign

~~~~

The **FACTS** are clear- take responsibility for *your*

Feelings **A**ctions **C**hoices **T**ime **S**pace